True words from the horse's mouth

There's a lot of belly laughs in this book and some pretty wild adventures me and Wilbur had that rocked the neighborhood. Like the time that blonde visiting next door fell for Wilbur and I played Cupid. Or the time old Wilb almost disgraced himself with a rich old Pillar of the Community. Then, of course, one night we was trying to do our patriotic duty and track down a dangerous criminal and the state troopers started shooting us up. Well, them stories are all here in this book. And a lot more.

So if you never before met a horse who can talk and who likes to drink his beer out of the bottle—why here's your chance with TV's best-loved star

The Original Mr. Ed

The
Original
Mr. Ed

by
Walter Brooks

Illustrated by Bob Bugg

BANTAM BOOKS  NEW YORK

THE ORIGINAL MR. ED

A Bantam Book / published January 1963

© *Copyright, 1963, by Dorothy R. Brooks*
Library of Congress Catalog Card Number: 63-8615
Published simultaneously in the United States and Canada.

Contents

Ed Shoots It Out

When anybody tells you that animals are just stupid and haven't any initiative you tell them about Wilbur Pope's horse. I guess you've heard about him. His name was Ed and he lived with Mr. and Mrs. Pope up in their little country place near Mt. Kisco. That is of course Ed lived in the barn. Mr. Pope had bought him so he could ride Saturdays and Sundays when Mrs. Pope was giving cocktail parties. And he was just as surprised as you or I would have been when he found out that Ed could talk.

Well of course Mr. Pope's first thought was of how he could cash in on Ed's gift. But Ed said nothing doing. So Mr. Pope had to give in and afterward he was glad he did. They ambled around Westchester stopping now and then for beer or to talk or take a nap under a tree and it settled down into a nice friendship.

Well one of Mr. Pope's neighbors was Senator Watson Kirby who had a big place on a hill overlooking several reservoirs. Senator Kirby had a noble head and the kind of eloquence that can take two from four and leave six and so he was being spoken of as the next governor. He had a daughter named Wilma who was a large healthy girl fond of the kind of sports that make you sweat. She usually wore breeches and stood with her feet apart when she talked to you. Mr. Pope liked her fine at first and when she dropped in one Sunday when she was out riding he talked to her and showed her Ed and by and by they went for a ride.

Well Miss Kirby was one of the hearty kind who say what they think and in the first half mile she told Mr. Pope what she thought. Were those people all your friends? she said and when Mr. Pope said Why yes didn't you like them? she said Don't they ever do anything week-ends but sit around and drink? What they need is more exercise and less whisky. You could do with a little more exercise yourself she said giving Mr. Pope's figure a critical looking over. Sud-

1

denly she startled Mr. Pope by exclaiming But man alive!
Why don't you pull up your girth? Why I could get both
hands under it. Eh? said Mr. Pope blinking at her and fum-
bling with his belt. Saddle girth said Miss Kirby. O said Mr.
Pope Why Ed don't like it tight. Pooh said Miss Kirby get
down and let me show you. You're riding for a bad fall.

So they both dismounted and Miss Kirby put one knee
against Ed's side and hauled on the strap until she had it
tight enough to suit her. You have to pull 'em tight she said.
A horse always swells himself up when you're saddling him.
Though strictly speaking she said eying Ed doubtfully I
don't think this is a horse at all. Look at the angle of that pastern. And those withers.

Mr. Pope who didn't know what a pastern was and for
whom withers were merely something that were better un-
wrung mumbled faintly.

When he had left Miss Kirby at her gate Mr. Pope steered
Ed homeward. We'll stop at Jake's and have some beer he
said. Get off and loosen that girth first said Ed. Do my eyes
look funny Wilb? I can feel 'em bulge and I don't believe I
can hold 'em in much longer. So Mr. Pope loosened the girth.
So I ain't strictly speaking a horse at all eh? said Ed. Well if
you ask me she ain't a girl. She's one of these sadists you
hear about. O she's all right said Mr. Pope. Yeah? said Ed.
Well you keep away from her Wilb. I don't like the way she
looks at you. Hungry. Like you was a lump of sugar.

Well it wasn't long before it began to look as if Ed was
right. Miss Kirby dropped in nearly every Sunday and then
she and Mr. Pope would take a ride which usually ended at
the Kirby place where there were comfortable chairs and
mild but cooling drinks. Mr. Pope rather enjoyed it. Miss
Kirby's conversation put no strain on the intellect as it was
all about horses and skiing and golf and mountain climbing
so that it was easy to follow.

The riding part wasn't so much fun. It was cross-country
and had fences and walls in it. The first time Ed was put at a
wall he refused point-blank. Damn it Wilbur he said I can't
jump over that thing. It's—well it's illegal. Go on! said Mr.
Pope What are you giving me? Well said Ed it's suicide. And
that's against the law ain't it? But by coaxing and threaten-
ing Mr. Pope finally got him to try it in a low place. After that
they did better and as Miss Kirby was usually some distance
ahead it was nearly always possible to scramble over or to
find a way around. But it was tiring.

Shouts of delight hailed the brilliantly
spotlighted embrace.

By August Miss Kirby was almost a daily caller and nearly all Mr. Pope's spare time was taken up with some form of sport. Not mild sport either. Even croquet at Miss Kirby's hands was a game to be pursued with steamy energy. The least strenuous was shooting at a mark with the .22 automatic rifle that Mr. Pope kept out in the barn to discourage rats.

But at last Mr. Pope struck. It was on a Sunday. A cross-country ride had been followed by eighteen holes of golf and after lunch at the Popes' they had had six sets of tennis at the Kirbys'. Mr. Pope lay gasping like a hooked trout on the grass. Come on Wilbur said Miss Kirby gaily. Sets are three all. We'll play it off and have a swim. More likely a funeral said Mr. Pope. No Wilma I'm through. I just can't keep it up. Nonsense my dear man! said Miss Kirby. Exercise never hurt anybody. You've sat around too many years lapping up highballs—that's what's the matter with you.

At that moment Senator Kirby came across the lawn. Ah Pope he said with a nod and then to his daughter Well child having a pleasant game? Wilbur wants to quit said Miss Kirby. You're dead right he does Wilbur said. Doesn't she ever get tired sir? She is a true Kirby said the senator. Sound old American stock Mr. Pope that plays as it works—strenuously. The pioneer strain sir that has never learned to cry Hold! Enough! Well you know this isn't a battle senator protested Mr. Kirby. You young fellows are too soft today said Mr. Kirby. Why when I was a young man . . .

On the way home Ed said to Mr. Pope I don't see why you played those extra sets after you said you wouldn't. I had to said Mr. Pope defensively. Anyway he went on I enjoy a certain amount of it. And I like Wilma. She's restful. Sure said Ed when she's sitting still. But just the same you look out for her. Go on—laugh. You wait and see.

Ed was worried about Mr. Pope all right but he was worried about himself too. He wanted the old peaceful days back. There was too much galloping and coming home in a lather and too many stone walls and woodchuck holes in these rides. Also he was uneasy about the suggestions Miss Kirby kept making that Mr. Pope buy a better horse. Wilbur's so darn easy to influence he said to himself. I guess I'd better take steps.

Well having been brought up in a stable Ed's methods were pretty direct. A couple of days later they were out riding and they came down through a wood lot into a pasture and there right in front of them was a large stern-looking bull. Miss Kirby said Hey Wilbur let's have a bullfight! and urged her horse into a canter right across the bull's bows. The bull put his head down and made a short run toward her and Miss Kirby laughed and circled around him and came across from the other side and the bull did it again. Gosh Ed what'll we do? said Mr. Pope. She'll get into trouble. But to his surprise Ed suddenly took the bit in his teeth and headed at a gallop straight for the bull. Olé shouted Ed. Here comes Wilbur the Matador!

Well of course Miss Kirby thought it was Mr. Pope who had entered into the spirit of things and she turned in the saddle to smile encouragement just as Ed swerved sharply and cannoned into her mount. Looking back as he swept by, Mr. Pope saw her topple from the saddle. Stop Ed! he yelled and tried to pull up and then as Ed kept right on going he kicked his feet free and dropped off. He ran back to Miss Kirby but she had kept hold of the rein and was already mounting. Quick! she said Get up behind me! But the bull instead of rushing them gazed for a moment with grandfatherly disapproval then turned aside and picked a mouthful of daisies.

Later Mr. Pope had it out with Ed. At least he tried to. But Ed said he hadn't meant anything. I just slipped he said. And anyway he said I didn't think you'd jump off. I suppose you didn't think Wilma'd fall off either said Mr. Pope. That bull might have killed her. Ed gave a hypocritical leer. Yes he said I should be more careful Wilbur. Dear me I don't know what came over me.

A couple of nights later the Popes had a party. Miss Kirby and Mr. Pope spent most of the evening at a ping-pong table up in the barn loft. About half past ten they stopped playing but halfway down the stairs Miss Kirby said Don't let's go out with all those people. Can't we sit somewhere quietly? I won't put the light on then said Mr. Pope. They felt their way down and Mr. Pope pulled an old bench out into the barn doorway and they sat down facing out toward the lawn. It was a hot night and most of the party was out on the lawn. We can see them and they can't see us said Miss Kirby. I like that don't you? Gosh! she said suddenly. What's that behind us? It's only Ed said Mr. Pope. I don't tie him up. It seems mean to confine him in a stall. Hello Ed he said. Hot tonight isn't it?

Ed didn't say anything. He had a plan. And the first time

Miss Kirby turned her head a little away from Mr. Pope he put it into operation. He stuck his head forward and kissed Miss Kirby lingeringly on the cheek.

O Wilbur! cried Miss Kirby. Don't be mushy! Mushy! exclaimed the stupefied Mr. Pope. But before he could say any more she threw her arms around him and embraced him with an athletic fervor that drove the breath out of him. O Wilbur! she said I *knew* that you cared! And at that moment Ed seized in his teeth the string of the big floodlight that hung over the barn door and pulled.

Shouts of delight hailed the brilliantly spotlighted embrace. The party crowded up around them as they sprang apart. Three to one on Wilbur! said some one. I'll take it said Jed Witherspoon. He hasn't a chance poor chap. Are you doing charades darlings? asked Mrs. Pope sweetly. Why didn't you tell us so we could guess? And then Mr. Pope found the light and turned it off.

Well Mr. Pope found Miss Kirby as she was getting into her car and she was pretty mad and said he ought to be horsewhipped for putting on the light but he finally persuaded her that he hadn't done it. No she said I guess I know you couldn't have. Not after kissing me like that. And let's be straight about this Wilbur. I've known for a long time that you cared for me. Now why don't you divorce Carlotta and marry me?

But good gosh sputtered Mr. Pope how can I—why I love Carlotta. Nonsense my dear man said Miss Kirby you can't. She's not your type. Besides I know you couldn't have kissed me as you did if you didn't care. Perhaps it did come as a shock to you. But you've got to face the truth Wilbur. You and I were made for each other. And she seized him and kissed him terrifyingly and then drove off.

Don't say it boss—don't say it said Ed as Mr. Pope came into the barn. I can't say it now replied Mr. Pope. There are too many people around. But I suppose you know you're looking the auction block right in the eye? I was only acting in your best interests said Ed. When you started hugging and kissing that wench—I started! exclaimed Mr. Pope. Why yes said Ed. Didn't you? I couldn't see very well. I don't know just what did happen said Mr. Pope. But I'm in a sweet mess *now*. And your putting on that light— I did it all for the best said Ed. I thought if Mrs. Pope saw you it would make her jealous and she'd keep the girl away from you. Instead of which—well she thought it was funny. He snickered. Well damn it Wilb it *was* funny. Bah! said Mr. Pope and left the barn.

Mrs. Pope didn't think it was so funny next day when Miss Kirby came to see her and asked her to give Mr. Pope up. She told Mr. Pope about it at dinner. She's crazy! said Mr. Pope bitterly. Well I don't know said Mrs. Pope. She seems quite sane to me. You can't be asking me to believe that she made the whole thing up? Of course she did said Mr. Pope. O no Wilbur Mrs. Pope said. This thing has been going on a long time. If you want to marry her I won't stand in your way. I've never interfered with you as I told her and if you want a divorce— O my heaven said Mr. Pope. I'm going over to see her father.

But the senator greeted him with a depressing cordiality. Ah Pope he said Well my girl tells me you've arranged it all between you. Congratulations my boy. Eh? said Mr. Pope. But Mr. Kirby don't you understand—I'm already married. I understand Pope I understand replied the senator. Your agitation does you credit. But divorce is no disgrace nowadays as long as it's accomplished quietly. And I understand your wife will offer no objection— But my dear senator interrupted Mr. Pope I don't want to—I haven't any intention of marrying Wilma.

What's this? demanded the senator and his brow began to build up voltage. If you've been playing fast and loose with my little girl— Then the brow cleared. I think I understand he said. But nowadays an uncontested divorce can have no effect on a young man's prospects. And surely if I in my position am not concerned you hardly need be. He laughed throatily. Tut-tut Mr. Pope he said. I hope you agree that my little girl—*our* little girl—must get what she wants?

Well Mr. Pope stayed a while but he didn't get anywhere so he went home and talked to Ed. That Wilma's a tough baby said Ed. You were right trying to work on her old man but you worked on him the wrong way. Now if he thought your wife might make a scandal— It's perfectly plain Carlotta wouldn't said Mr. Pope. I'm not so sure said Ed. But anyway— Well the guy wants to be governor doesn't he? I think I got an idea. Well said Mr. Pope what is it? I got to think it out said Ed. By the way Wilbur I saw a couple rats last night. Is that rifle of yours loaded? Mr. Pope took the rifle down from its hook. Yes he said. Then he looked suspiciously at Ed. I hope you're not planning any shooting? he said. Me shoot? said Ed. With hoofs? Don't be silly.

Mr. Pope alleged pressing business and spent the next three nights in town. The first two evenings Mrs. Pope went out but the third she stayed home and went to bed early. About eleven o'clock Ed got busy. He had stolen a pink felt hat of Mrs. Pope's that she had left in the garden a day or two before and he got that and then he carefully took down the rat rifle from the hook and with these two things held firmly in his mouth he started for the Kirbys'.

He came through the Kirby property from the back and worked up close to the side of the house under cover of the shrubbery. There was a light in Miss Kirby's room but the downstairs rooms were dark. Ed dropped the hat on the lawn and propped the gun against a stone bench and pushed it around until it pointed at the window next the lighted one. He managed to get the safety catch off with his teeth and then he stood still and watched the window which was open although the shade was down. Pretty soon Miss Kirby's shadow moved across it and Ed called in a high falsetto voice Wilma!

Miss Kirby raised the shade and looked out. Who is that? she said. O there you are you husband snatcher you! yelled Ed. Take that! And he leaned down and pushed the rifle trigger with his nose. There was a bang and a crash of glass and Miss Kirby herself let out a very creditable yell. And Ed gave a wild shriek of laughter and then trotted off into the bushes where he hid and watched.

Pretty soon lights flashed on and Miss Kirby and her father and a couple of disheveled servants came tumbling out with flashlights and pokers and walking sticks. Soon one of the servants found the rifle and the hat. Heavens! said Miss Kirby. That's Carlotta Pope's hat. That's Wilbur's rat rifle too.

The senator came down and examined the relics. Mrs. Pope's? he said. But child you assured me— He stopped and pulled himself together and then managed a hollow laugh. All right Hicks he said. You and Wallace go in. I know all about it. I'd forgotten for the moment. It's just a—a bet. A joke.

When the servants had gone he said to his daughter You heard that shriek. The woman is plainly crazy. Good heavens if I'd had any idea of this— But there must be no scandal. But I must find Wilbur Miss Kirby said and tell him. I think you will not be seeing Wilbur again said the senator. Come in at once. So they went in and Ed went home.

The next evening Mr. Pope came out. Mrs. Pope acted funny at dinner he thought. But at last she said Queer the Kirbys dashing off on a South American cruise so suddenly wasn't it? The senator called me up to tell me. Said he thought it might set my mind at rest. You mean they've really gone? said Mr. Pope. Mrs. Pope showed him the item in the evening paper. My gosh what a break! he said. Then he looked at her mournfully. Or isn't it a break for you? Mrs. Pope got up and came over and sat on the arm of his chair. Darling she said sometimes I think you're just a little stupid. And she kissed him. When she was through Mr. Pope said dazedly Gosh! Yeah.

Later he went out to see Ed and tell him the news. Well now that's something said Ed. Yeah said Mr. Pope and how is that idea of yours coming? Idea? said Ed. O I gave that up. Nothing to it. Mr. Pope looked at him suspiciously. You act funny Ed he said. And the Kirbys dash off without any explanation— O sure sure said Ed bitterly. If something happens you blame it on me and if nothing happens you blame that on me too. Gosh I don't know why I don't join the navy.

O. K. Ed said Mr. Pope. My apologies. I've got some new Bourbon in the house. I'll bring you out a bottle.

The Midnight Ride of Mr. Ed

One good thing about having a horse that can talk is that there's always somebody to discuss your personal worries with. Wilbur Pope talked over nearly everything with his horse Ed—even things he couldn't talk over with Mrs. Pope. He felt that a horse could be more objective about some things than a wife could. Of course Ed wasn't any too sympathetic sometimes. He was pretty hard-boiled. He never let the conventions inhibit his actions and he wasn't much of a hand for the nuances either. Hell Wilbur he'd say I admire your good manners all right but they're a terrible handicap. When a guy insults you you give him the soft answer. Me I kick him in the stomach. Thank heaven I wasn't brought up right.

So when Mr. Pope told Ed that Mrs. Pope's Aunt Edith was coming for another week's visit Ed just said Well tell her she can't come. But I can't do that Ed said Mr. Pope because you see—well I just can't. What's she got on you? said Ed. You don't understand said Mr. Pope. It isn't that she's got anything on me. But after all she's Carlotta's aunt. And Carlotta's fond of her. Besides she's trustee for the money Carlotta inherited from her other aunt. I thought it would boil down to money sooner or later said Ed. Well said Mr. Pope Carlotta gets a couple hundred a month from it and if Aunt Edith got sore she could cut it off. She has complete control. And it would mean Carlotta's doing without a lot of clothes and other extras. It does seem little enough to do—for me to be pleasant to Aunt Edith.

Sounds all right when you put it that way said Ed. Only I guess you forgot Wilbur that you told me about how this aunt woman threatened to cut the money all off last year unless your wife divorced you. No I didn't forget that said Mr. Pope. She's sort of down on men. When she was young she had a lot of money and the fortune hunters were after her and the worst one in the lot pretty near got her. She

*"At the sight of Ed and his rider
they yelled and dived. . . ."*

found out in time that he was suspected of having murdered his first wife. Too bad said Ed but there's always some busybody around. So you see went on Mr. Pope she'd try to break up any marriage that Carlotta made. And when she heard I'd said I had a horse that could talk— You did kind of stick your neck out on that put in Ed. I wouldn't have said Mr. Pope if you'd backed me up. But that's neither here nor there now. The trouble is I suppose she'll start the old divorce campaign again and if I could only think of some excuse to be away while she's here it would be a lot easier all around.

H'm said Ed. Don't you have to go out and see that client of yours in Peoria? But Mr. Pope said no—he couldn't stay there a week and anyway Mrs. Pope might find out. H'm said Ed again and then he looked at Mr. Pope and said You know Wilb I can't ever seem to think very good when I'm thirsty. O K said Mr. Pope and he went in the house and came back with half a bottle of Scotch. Ought to be enough here to give us an idea he said.

After the second drink Ed said You know Wilb I've made a discovery. I've discovered what makes the Scotchman talk that kind of dialect. It's from having a bottle in your mouth. Here take a swig and try saying Ha'e ye no' anither bottle? So Mr. Pope tried it. Why you're right he said and then he started on Ye banks and braes o' bonnie Doon but only got to the second verse when Ed said Hey! My turn! So Mr. Pope handed over the bottle and Ed tried It's a braw bricht moonlicht nicht.

When the bottle was empty Mr. Pope said hopefully Well Ed have you thought of anything? Sure I have said Ed. Why don't you get your friend Dr. Kendall to send you to the hospital? By George said Mr. Pope I believe you've got it! You needn't act so shook up about it said Ed. Why don't we ride over and see him right away and we can stop at Barney's for some beer. I'm still thirsty.

So they rode over. When's your aunt coming? Dr. Kendall asked and when Mr. Pope told him next Friday he said Well we can throw you in for observation. We can't let you have anything serious because you don't want to worry Carlotta. I guess bursitis is the thing for you. We'll make it your shoulder. You'd better begin complaining about its being lame and Thursday it gets so sore you can't move it and you come over and I'll send you to this new hospital we've got out here. It's only a few minutes' drive from Mt.

Kisco so it'll be handy for Carlotta. Will she bring the aunt to see you? Not if I groan a lot said Mr. Pope. She hasn't much patience with sick people. Groaning's O. K. said Dr. Kendall. You'd be in some pain. And you ought to have a temperature. But we'll arrange that. Otherwise you'll have nothing to do but sit around your room and keep your shoulder quiet. Only one thing—when you go into the hospital try not to smell so strong of beer.

Well everything went fine and Thursday night Mrs. Pope drove Mr. Pope and a couple of dozen detective stories over to the hospital. She was so sympathetic that he felt pretty ashamed and would have backed out but of course it was too late. I'm sorry not to be on hand to welcome Aunt Edith he said. But you just go ahead with your plans with her and don't bother about me. I'll have to said Mrs. Pope but I'll get over every day.

Well the first two days were wonderful. His room was on the ground floor and there was nothing to do but sit in the window and read and wait for the next meal to be brought in. He had put his arm in a sling so he wouldn't forget and use it when anybody was in the room. He always had a hot water bottle handy and when it was about time for the nurse to come in and take his temperature he would put it on his shoulder and lean his cheek against it and this ran the thermometer up so he appeared suitably feverish. Dr. Kendall ran in and brought gossip and stories and nurses flitted in and out with different gossip but the same stories and it was all very much like the office only without the responsibility. Mr. Pope felt very happy and carefree.

But that did not last long. On the third day just after breakfast he went to get something out of his bag on the wardrobe shelf and he was standing there with both arms over his head when a nurse came in. My goodness Mr. Pope said the nurse can you get your arm up like that? Mr. Pope was pretty confused and he stammered and said well he guessed it was a lot better. The nurse said it certainly must be and then she told him that Dr. Kendall was ill and wouldn't be in to see him that morning but that Dr. Coleman who was taking his work would be in. And by and by Dr. Coleman came. He was a dark suspicious-looking young man and there was a false heartiness about him that worried Mr. Pope. I can't trust this guy he said to himself.

Dr. Coleman had Mr. Pope's chart in his hand and he looked from it to Mr. Pope and back again as if he was comparing a police handbill with a criminal in the line-up. Arm's a lot better this morning the nurse tells me he said. Seems to be said Mr. Pope. What's wrong with Bill? Acute appendicitis said Dr. Coleman. He was at a party in town last night and was taken sick and shot right into St. Luke's and operated on. They got it in time fortunately. And without pausing for comment he whipped out a thermometer and jabbed it into Mr. Pope's mouth. Mr. Pope was resentful. Darned unfair! he thought. Unfair to organized deception.

Now let's have a look at that shoulder said Dr. Coleman and he snatched the thermometer and after glancing at it began manipulating Mr. Pope's arm. Mr. Pope tried wincing a few times but noticed that Dr. Coleman's eyebrows went up each time and gave it up. After all he had had no instructions on that point from Dr. Kendall.

Well doctor he said how soon can you get me out of here? O a few days I think said Dr. Coleman. You're perfectly contented? Getting a good rest eh? Mr. Pope said he was. So Dr. Coleman said he'd stop in tomorrow and nodded to the nurse and they went out. But the door didn't latch and as it swung ajar again Mr. Pope heard him say to the nurse Does Dr. Kendall ever send any psychiatric patients to this hospital? The nurse said something and Dr. Coleman said H'm. Then he said Isn't this the Mr. Pope who— But the door swung shut and Mr. Pope didn't hear any more.

Well Mr. Pope was kind of worried. Maybe I ought to have told the guy he said to himself. But he's so stuffy he'd think Bill had been unethical or something in sending me here. I can't let Bill down.

Pretty soon Mrs. Pope and Aunt Edith came. Aunt Edith was large and smooth and encrusted with diamonds. She said she was sorry he was ill. Mr. Pope shifted his position and groaned. Painful? said Aunt Edith hopefully. Mr. Pope smiled bravely. It's much better he said. Isn't it too bad about Bill? said Mrs. Pope. Yes said Mr. Pope but Coleman says he's going to be all right. Aunt Edith knows Dr. Coleman. Isn't that nice? said Mrs. Pope. He's the son of a very old friend said Aunt Edith. A brilliant young man and very well connected. And she told them about Dr. Coleman's connections.

Mr. Pope groaned some more and Aunt Edith got restless and said finally Well Carlotta we mustn't tire Wilbur. So they left.

Late that evening Mr. Pope was reading when somebody outside the window said Psst! Good Lord said Mr. Pope is that you Ed? and he jumped up and went to the window. Hi Wilb said Ed. Thought I'd slip my halter and trot over and see if I could find you. I stuck my nose in every window on this floor. Boy! There's a guy two doors down in blue pajamas—he'll never be the same. And Ed began to laugh. Sssh! said Mr. Pope. O K said Ed. Look Wilb—I thought maybe you'd like to sneak out for a ride. A midnight ride to get some beer like Longfellow says. There's a nurse out at the desk now—cute little trick. Whyn't you ring your bell and get her in here and we can take her along. I can carry you both. But hold on a minute he said. You can't get out—this window's barred. Well I'll be darned said Mr. Pope I hadn't noticed that. But anyway Ed I couldn't go. They'd miss me. How's everything at home?

Not so good said Ed. That's one reason I came over. I think you ought to come home Wilbur. Aunt Edith is certainly stirring up the mud. She got your wife to ask that guy Coleman to dinner tonight. He brought up that old business about your bragging how I could talk. I was just outside the window—I'm keeping an eye on your interests Wilb. Anyway he was kind of hinting around—in a sort of a nasty joking way you know—and then auntie jumps in with the whole story. Your wife tried to shush her but auntie says Now Carlotta it's as well to face the facts. I've had a little talk with Dr. Coleman. He says there's nothing wrong with Wilbur's arm. And of course as he can't talk to Dr. Kendall he thinks it's important to find out just why Dr. Kendall sent Wilbur to the hospital.

And then this Coleman squirts his poison. He says as far as he can see you are O K *physically*—and then he kind of pauses and says You see Mrs. Pope I am responsible now and if there are any little ways in which Mr. Pope has seemed to you—well—eccentric— Well there's one thing I'll say for your wife Wilb—she certainly sticks up for you when you're not around. Boy did she put that guy through the mangle! They came out on the porch about then so I had to duck and didn't hear any more.

Well said Mr. Pope to tell you the truth Ed I don't like this much. Neither do I said Ed. They've got you headed for the booby hatch if you ask me. Why don't you get out of here? I couldn't get by the desk tonight without a row said Mr. Pope. I'll wait till tomorrow and have it out with

Coleman. Maybe that's best said Ed. Well I ought to start back. I want to have another peek at that fat guy in the blue pajamas. You'd have died if you could have seen him Wilb. I don't want him to see *you* Ed said Mr. Pope. You'll get us in trouble. I won't let him see me said Ed. I just want to give him a giggle. Like this. And Ed giggled.

Well just as he did so although Mr. Pope didn't know it a nurse came into the room. She saw Mr. Pope's back as he stood at the window and she heard that shrill inhuman giggle and she put the two together and fled. Mr. Pope shushed Ed and got back into bed just as she came in again. There was an older nurse with her. Did you—we thought we heard you laughing said the nurse uncertainly. O yes said Mr. Pope I heard it too. Out in the grounds somewhere I think. They looked at him steadily and the older nurse said It's pretty late—oughtn't you to try to get some rest? Perhaps you're right said Mr. Pope. So they cranked his bed flat and put out the light. But when they went out they left the door open.

Well Dr. Coleman came in early next morning and Mr. Pope went right at him. Look here Coleman he said do you think I'm crazy or something? My dear fellow! said Dr. Coleman laughing. What an odd question! My shoulder's all right now said Mr. Pope. I suggest that you let me go home. As far as your shoulder goes that's a perfectly reasonable suggestion said Dr. Coleman. But you see I'd have to have Dr. Kendall's approval. I hope to talk to him tomorrow. Well Mr. Pope argued but Dr. Coleman was firm. Another day's rest won't hurt your shoulder a bit he said.

Yeah? said Mr. Pope when he had gone. Well I'm going anyway. But when he went to get his clothes they weren't there. Good Lord he said this is serious! To go wandering around Westchester in pajamas would be just handing his sanity to Aunt Edith on a silver platter so he started another detective story. The thing to do was wait and tell Mrs. Pope the truth when she came that afternoon. But she didn't come. Instead Aunt Edith showed up. Carlotta wasn't feeling well she said so she'd come over to see if there was anything he wanted.

I want to get out of here said Mr. Pope but this man Coleman's acting very strange about it. He's even had them hide my clothes. Well Wilbur said Aunt Edith I do hope you're not going to be difficult about it. I felt it was so sensible of you to come in here voluntarily. It is unfortunate that you have taken such a dislike to Dr. Coleman. He says that if you could only bring yourself to be as frank with him as you have been with Dr. Kendall it would be so much better for you.

I see said Mr. Pope—you all think that I told Bill I was cuckoo. Then he laughed. I must say he said you were rather courageous to come here. I suppose Coleman told you I wouldn't get violent. But frankly I don't think he understands my case very well. Sometimes you know it just comes over me all at once. Mr. Pope glared at her and got slowly to his feet. I remember he said for how many years you've been trying to break up our marriage and then— He raised his hands slowly and Aunt Edith gave a low howl and bolted.

That was a silly thing to do said Mr. Pope to himself. Now what in blazes can I do? But the day dragged on and he didn't think of anything. So he read some more and had dinner and at last at nine o'clock he heard a Psst! and Ed was at the window.

Look Wilb said Ed you got to get home right away. That aunt woman and the doc have been working on your wife. He's there to dinner again. And she's been cryin' all afternoon. That doc's been telling about a lot of cases just like yours—people that thought spirits talked to 'em and so on. It's pretty convincing. Gosh I have my doubts about you now myself. But here—get busy on these window bars. I brought you this screwdriver.

Well it took half an hour but they weren't interrupted and as soon as the bottom screws were out they bent two bars apart and Mr. Pope was off and away. Ed went cross-country and nobody saw them. Boy! he said I'm glad to get you out of that place! We'll throw a scare into Aunt Edith that'll explode her pompadour. No funny business now Ed said Mr. Pope. Eh? said Ed. No no of course not. Just drop me off at the side door so I can sneak in and get some clothes on said Mr. Pope. O sure sure said Ed.

But Ed had his own ideas about how things should be done. Aunt Edith and Dr. Coleman were sitting on the porch talking in low tones when there came the thud of hoofs on turf and a shrill screaming neigh. They jumped up and then as Ed with his pajama-clad rider clattered up the steps toward them they yelled in unison and dived—Aunt Edith under the porch hammock and Dr. Coleman over the rail into the night.

Well Mrs. Pope had been up in her room and she rushed down just as Mr. Pope having sent Ed off to the stable was trying to coax Aunt Edith out from under the hammock. Wilbur! she exclaimed and threw herself into his arms. It's all right darling he said. That fool Coleman wouldn't let me out of there so I got someone to bring Ed over. Look— you don't think I'm cuckoo do you? O Wilbur said Mrs. Pope I don't know what to think! It's—it's so confusing and queer! I can straighten it all out said Mr. Pope but I must get dressed.

So he went upstairs. While he dressed he heard a good deal of talking and moving around in Aunt Edith's room which was on the ground floor under his bedroom and when he went down Mrs. Pope came out to him. I don't know what to say Wilbur she said. I wish you hadn't come back in quite this way. It looks— Sure said Mr. Pope it looks queer all right. But Bill can explain when he gets well. I got him to send me to the hospital so I wouldn't have to be here while Aunt Edith was staying with you. Only we can't tell them that. It wouldn't be fair to Bill. But what on earth *can* we tell them? said Mrs. Pope. We'll have to stick to it that I really did have a bum arm said Mr. Pope. You try to quiet Aunt Edith down while I go out and rub Ed down. We galloped all the way.

Ed wasn't in the stable but Mr. Pope found him finally behind some shrubbery peering into the open window of Aunt Edith's room. Come come Ed he whispered you ought to have more dignity than to be going in for this Peeping Tom stuff. Gosh you certainly messed things up! I'm afraid I did Wilb murmured Ed. But do a little peeping yourself. Listen!

Aunt Edith was standing in the room and as Mr. Pope crept closer he saw the door open and Dr. Coleman come in. I got Dr. Bancroft on the phone said Dr. Coleman and I'll drive over to the hospital now and pick him up. But said Aunt Edith you can't leave us alone in the house with that madman! I'm sure he's quite harmless said Dr. Coleman. You just stay in your room. But he must be put under restraint immediately! said Aunt Edith. Of course said Dr. Coleman but Bancroft will have to see him first with me. You just leave it to me.

Ed nudged Mr. Pope and they walked over to the stable. Looks like they'd got you in the grinder Wilbur said Ed. Anyway until Kendall gets on his feet again. Say listen. I've got an idea. You go on in the house and leave this to me said Ed. And as it was all he could do Mr. Pope did.

Mrs. Pope was in the living room and Mr. Pope sat down beside her. Thank heaven *you* don't think I'm a lunatic anyway Carlotta he said. Well you've certainly acted like one said Mrs. Pope and what on earth we're going to do about this psychiatrist that Dr. Coleman's bringing— The worst thing is she said that you threatened Aunt Edith. Mr Pope remarked gloomily that the whole situation looked like the worst thing to him.

Pretty soon a car swished into the drive and a minute later Dr. Coleman came into the room followed by a tall gray-haired man. The Popes got up and Dr. Coleman introduced them to Dr. Bancroft who fixed piercing eyes on Mr. Pope and said Now suppose we just sit down and talk things over quietly. And at that moment from behind the closed door of Aunt Edith's room there came a high inhuman giggle followed by a shriek.

Good heavens! said Dr. Bancroft and Dr. Coleman rushed to the door and tried to pull it open but it was locked on the inside. And then again came the insane giggle followed by the sound of a gabbling voice—or two voices—it was hard to tell. Then the crash of an overturned table and frantic rattling of the doorknob and the door flew open and a disheveled Aunt Edith plunged into Dr. Coleman's arms. O doctor that terrible horse! she panted. He said things—horrible things. And then *laughed!* O! and her eyes turned up and she fainted.

Dr. Bancroft stepped quickly to the door and looked in. Then he turned with raised eyebrows and a shrug to Dr. Coleman who was bending over Aunt Edith. Nothing there he said. Of course there's nothing there said Mr. Pope. I'm very sorry this happened gentleman he went on. We've rather tried to protect Aunt Edith. Even to the extent he said with a faint smile of my almost having to take the rap for her. You see he went on she's always had this odd idea about a horse. The things she told you about me Dr. Coleman were merely a transference. I don't know much about these things but as I get it she transfers her own hallucinations to me somehow.

Dr. Bancroft nodded at him. O yes he said it's not at all uncommon. Well Coleman if she's coming around I think —unless Mr. Pope would like us to stay for a little—? Not at all necessary said Mr. Pope. Carlotta will get her to bed and she'll be quite all right in the morning. I'm sure she will said Dr. Bancroft who was plainly anxious to go. Come Coleman he said sharply and the younger man still looking very puzzled said an unwilling good night and they left.

When Mr. Pope came back from the door Aunt Edith was sitting up and Mrs. Pope was holding her hand. You must get me into town she was saying. I wouldn't spend another night in that room. Now Aunt Edith said Mr. Pope I do hope you're not going to be difficult. You know he said I'm afraid Dr. Coleman feels that you haven't been perhaps any more frank with him than I was. Funny isn't it how the horse sort of came home to roost?

Aunt Edith glared at him. I begin to see she said tightly. That horse that spoke to me—it was some abominable hoax. Well I warn you Wilbur— Let me warn *you* Aunt Edith interrupted Mr. Pope. We have two doctors—one a psychiatrist—as witnesses that you claim to have been insulted by a horse. In that case I think any further pressure on Carlotta to get rid of me would be most unwise. Also there's another point. A person who hears horses talking would hardly be considered capable of administering a trust fund. I suggest therefore that it might also be unwise to withhold on any pretext any part of the full amount of interest earned for Carlotta each quarter.

Well Aunt Edith continued to glare but Mr. Pope faced her calmly and after a minute she threw up her hands. Help me pack my bag Carlotta she said. I'm leaving.

When Mrs. Pope had taken Aunt Edith to the station Mr. Pope went out to see Ed. Well I've got to hand it to you Ed he said and told him what had happened. But what did you say to her? he asked. Nothing said Ed I just stuck my head through the window and waggled my ears and gave her the old giggle. But you said something insisted Mr. Pope—something horrible. She said you did. Yeah? said Ed. Well maybe I did Wilb. You know how I am—always polished and courtly. And being alone with a lady in her bedroom— well maybe I did pay her a compliment or two. Gosh! said Mr. Pope I hope not. I know your compliments. Ed winked at him. You don't know this one Wilb he said and you never will. Mr. Pope decided that it was better to let the matter drop.

His Royal Harness

Wilbur had a cousin named George Hubbard who lived in Washington. Mr. Hubbard had two little girls named Jean and Silvie. He also had a wife named Margery who felt that she had married beneath her. She felt this because she was a Destinn, which is quite a name in the part of the country she came from, though I can't remember where it is. But the little girls were nice.

So one summer they came up to visit the Popes in Mt. Kisco. The Popes gave parties for them and took them around to their friends' houses, and they all had a good time because there's a lot going on in Westchester if you're popular, and the Popes were. The men liked Mrs. Pope because she always said more than she meant, and the women liked Mr. Pope because he always said less. The men liked Mr. Pope too because he wasn't always watching Mrs. Pope. I don't know whether the women liked Mrs. Pope or not. They said they did.

Usually when there were parties and things Mr. Pope would sneak off and he and Ed would amble around the country and have a few beers, and talk about the kind of things people talk about when they're having a few beers. And Ed's talk—as you'd expect a horse's to be—was kind of racy. But with house guests there Mr. Pope had to stick to the parties, and this left Ed sort of out of things. It also left the two little girls out of things. And naturally they drifted together.

The barn where Mr. Pope garaged Ed was a regular barn complete with stalls and watering trough and mice. It was kind of a funny thing to find in the grounds of a suburban home, but then I guess that a horse that can talk is a funny thing to find there too. It was pretty clean though, because Ed was fussy about some things and he insisted on Mr. Pope's having it swept out twice a week. So Mrs. Hubbard

didn't mind having the little girls play there. Of course
the little girls loved it.

Well one day they were playing there and Ed was in his
stall munching oats.

"My, that horse makes a lot of noise munching," said
Silvie.

"I guess he hasn't got very good manners," said Jean. "I
expect we ought to speak to him about it."

So they climbed up and hung over the low partition between the stalls and looked at him. Ed liked the little girls
and he liked to listen to their talk, but you know how it is
yourself—if you are eating and somebody talks to you, you'd
rather listen to your own munching than to the wittiest
conversation in the world. So he hadn't heard what they
said. And when Jean said, "My mother says it isn't polite to
make noises when you eat," he didn't hear that either. But
they looked so cute that he stopped munching and winked
at them. And instead of being surprised they laughed and
winked back.

"Nice horsie," said Silvie, and reached over and patted
his neck. "I bet he isn't a horse at all," she said. "I bet he has
been turned into a horse by a wicked wizard."

"Mother says those stories aren't true," said Jean. "She
says they're absurd."

"Pooh!" said Silvie, "I bet he's a prince, and I bet he's
under a spell."

"If he was a prince he wouldn't chew so loud," said Jean.

"If I was a princess," said Silvie, "I would chew loud. I
would chew so loud you could hear me all over the palace.
And nobody could stop me because I would be the princess."

Being able to talk was pretty tough on Ed because he was
sociable and liked gossip, but he knew that if it got around
that he could talk he'd end up on the vaudeville stage, or
being investigated by psychologists. And he wanted a quiet
life. But he thought if I talk to these kids and they tell
about it nobody'll believe them. They'll think they're just
making up fairy stories. So he shook his head and said,
"Dear, dear! Then I guess you would never do for me."

The two little girls stared at him and their eyes were as
round as doorknobs, and Jean said, "Good gracious" and
Silvie said, "O he is a prince, he is a prince!"

"Don't be silly," said Jean severely. "Just because he can
talk don't mean he is a prince. Lots of horses can talk."

"O is that so!" said Silvie, and Jean said, "Yes that is so!"

"I bet he isn't a horse at all. He's been
turned into a horse by a wicked wizard."

"Well I'm going to ask him," said Silvie.

They had been acting as if Ed wasn't there, but now Silvie dropped down from the partition and went around into Ed's stall and said, "You are a prince, aren't you?" And Ed said, "Yes."

"There, smarty," said Silvie, and Jean said, "Well I think a prince ought to have better manners."

"Well you see," said Ed, "it's kind of hard to know how to act. There's a set of manners for princes, and there's a set of manners for horses, and while in one way of looking at it I'm a prince, in another I'm a horse. Seems to me it causes less talk if I use horse manners. Of course when I'm released from this spell and changed back into my rightful form, I'll use prince's manner like I was taught in my father's palace. My father wouldn't stand for any of that munching—no indeed."

"Well what did you mean about I wouldn't do for you?" said Silvie.

"Why it's a long story," said Ed, "but if you haven't any bridge parties or other genteel riots on this afternoon—?"

"No, no, we want to hear," said the little girls.

"Well it's this way," said Ed. "My father, old King Jumbo, was one of the nicest men that ever lived. His people loved him and he was a whiz at his job. But like most people he wasn't satisfied with the job he had—he wanted to do something more. He wanted to be a magician. And that would have been all right too, only he wasn't a good magician. His spells always went wrong, and his incantations were something terrible. He took lessons from some of the highest priced wizards in the country, but they all told him he had no future in magic and he'd better stick to ruling. The only trick he was any good at was taking rabbits out of a hat, and he was so pleased that he could do it that he kept it up until the palace was overrun with them. When you went to bed there were rabbits under your pillow, and when you got up to dress there were rabbits in your shoes. So he cast a spell to make them disappear, but something went wrong, as usual, and they all changed into elephants. My father was kind of discouraged."

"My goodness," said Jean, "what did you do?"

"Well," said Ed, "we all had to go down to my aunt's to stay that night, and my father wanted to try another spell to get them out, but everybody said we'd had enough magic. So the prime minister had an idea. You know there's nothing

elephants like so much as a parade. So he got out the royal
band and a regiment of the palace guards and marched
them past a few times. All the elephants rushed to the windows, and then when the parade went down the street they
all piled out and followed it. The band marched them
through the city gate and off down the road, and we never
saw any of them again. Of course it was too bad to lose our
band, but it was better than having the palace full of elephants."

"Mercy!" said Silvie, "I bet King Jumbo never tried any
magic again."

"He did, though," said Ed. "That's how I got turned into
a horse. You see when I grew up I wanted to be a policeman.
But the king wanted me to be a soldier. I don't like fighting
much, and I thought it would be more fun to direct traffic,
and tell people to move on and so on. And in a policeman's
business there's always a lot of free liq—that is free liquorice
and candy and such. But my father was pretty set, and when
I wouldn't give in, he tried magic. He had a spell that
would turn me into a soldier. But he got it wrong again, and
I was turned into a horse.

"Well I don't know if you have ever turned anybody into a
horse, but if you have you know it's almost impossible to get
them back again. The king called in all the C.P.W.'s in the
realm—"

"What's C.P.W.'s?" asked Jean.

"Certified Public Wizards," said Ed. "But they all agreed
there was nothing to be done. When I married, they said I'd
turn back into a prince. 'But how can he get anybody to
marry him if he's a horse?' said the king. 'That's his problem,' said the wizards. So I went out into the world to see if
I could find a bride.

"Well of course most girls won't believe I'm a prince. And
those that do there's mostly something wrong with."

"There isn't anything wrong with me," said Silvie.

"If I married you you'd be a princess," said Ed, "and I
wouldn't want a princess that chewed so loud they heard her
all over the place—I mean palace."

"You could marry me," said Jean, "and Silvie could
come to the wedding and not eat anything."

"Maybe you could marry us both," said Silvie, "and Jean
could have her meals with you, and I could have mine with
the servants. I like that better anyway. Jean could be the

princess to eat with, and I could be the princess to be in love with."

Well Ed was pondering this bigamous suggestion when Mrs. Hubbard came into the barn. "Come, children," she said, "you must get ready for dinner." So she took them into the house, and they chattered all the way about the horse they had met who was really an enchanted prince. Mrs. Hubbard didn't pay much attention for a while, and then she said, "That will do children. Don't be absurd." So the little girls knew what that meant, and they shut up.

But they were too excited to keep still very long, and at dinner they began again.

"Mother," said Jean, "do you suppose he would really turn into a prince if he got married?"

"It would be awful if he didn't," said Silvie, "because then you would be married to a horse."

"Did he really say in so many words that he was a prince?" asked Mr. Pope.

But before they could answer Mrs. Hubbard said, frowning, "Don't encourage them please, Wilbur. I do wish people wouldn't tell them these dreadful fairy stories."

"But this isn't a fairy story, mother," said Silvie,—"I mean it's really true. The horse did tell us—"

"That's quite enough," said Mrs. Hubbard angrily. "Go to your room—both of you."

"Well I must say, Margie," said Mr. Pope, when they had gone, "I don't see what harm there is in their making up a fairy story."

"I detest such stories," said Mrs. Hubbard. "I want my children to grow up with some sense of reality. You heard Silvie. Swearing up and down that the horse told her that stuff!"

"Margie's right," said Mr. Hubbard weakly.

"Well I still don't see," began Mr. Pope, but Mrs. Pope interrupted. "You'd better let people discipline their own children, Wilbur," she said. So Mr. Pope shut up.

Well, Mr. Pope knew that Ed was at the bottom of all this, but he didn't get a chance to talk to him for a few days because the Hubbards had to be entertained. And in the meantime the little girls were playing in the barn, and getting a lot more information about palace affairs in the reign of Jumbo VIII, and about the charm and achievements of his son Prince Ed. And the children told their mother, because they believed that continued assertions of an incredible fact would win belief. But in this case it only won spankings. Mrs. Hubbard got good and mad finally, and after she had spanked them she said, "Now children, I am going to give you one last chance to tell the truth. It's bad enough to tell a lie, but to persist in it to your own mother when she knows it cannot be true is a very serious matter. So I warn you. If you admit you were telling a lie we'll say no more about it, but if you still persist, I shan't let you go to your Aunt Caroline's this fall. Now did the horse tell you these things, or did you make them up?"

Well the little girls had been looking forward to the visit to their aunt's for a long time. They thought for a minute, and then Jean said, "You want us to tell you the truth, don't you, mother?"

"Certainly," said Mrs. Hubbard.

"Well then," said Jean, and stopped.

"The horse *did* tell us," said Silvie.

"Yes he did," said Jean.

"Very well," said Mrs. Hubbard coldly, and she went out and shut the door.

Well Mrs. Hubbard was pretty upset, and at dinner she told the Popes about it. "To think," she said, "that children of mine could be such determined little liars!"

"It seems to be a common delusion that that horse of Wilbur's is something of a conversationalist," said Mrs. Pope. "Wilbur tried to convince a number of people that he could talk."

"Sure, he talks," said Mr. Pope, "though I doubt if he has royal blood in him."

"Well I don't think it's very funny," said Mrs. Hubbard, looking suspiciously at Mr. Pope.

"My dear Margie!" said Mr. Pope. "If I chose to believe that Ed could talk, what harm did it do? It was true for me. So I wasn't lying when I said so. I think it's the same with the kids. They're not really lying."

"I'm afraid you're too metaphysical for me," said Mrs. Hubbard. "A lie's a lie."

"And if you begin believing such things," put in Mr. Hubbard, "your sense of reality's gone. Pretty soon you don't know what's true and what's false. And you make a fool of yourself."

"That's true," said Mr. Pope, "but there are worse things. God deliver me from a person who has never made a fool of himself."

"Well I don't understand you," said Mrs. Hubbard. "I certainly don't make a fool of myself. And so I suppose you find me ridiculous, Wilbur?"

"Not ridiculous," said Mr. Pope. "But I think a person who occasionally makes a fool of himself is more human, and possibly a pleasanter person to have around."

"Well really, Wilbur!" said Mrs. Pope, and Mrs. Hubbard put down her napkin and got up. "I'm sorry you feel I'm not a pleasant person to have around," she said. "I'm afraid I don't understand you, Wilbur. When I'm only trying to do what is right for the children. I think if you'll excuse me, Carlotta—" And she left the room.

"My gosh, George, I'm sorry," said Mr. Pope. "I was only talking generalities." Mr. Hubbard said embarrassedly that he understood. "But Margie's disturbed about this thing," he said. "I think pershaps—" And he left the room too.

And then Mrs. Pope got up and said disgustedly, "Well I guess you fixed *that!*" and followed them. So Mr. Pope went out to talk to Ed.

"Hello, Wilb," said Ed, "where've you been these last few days? Ain't mad at me or anything?"

"No," said Mr. Pope, "I was just diffident about coming out here without a royal summons, now you're the heir to a throne."

"O you've heard about that, eh?" said Ed. "Well don't let that worry you. Us kings and princes are pretty democratic these days. Why I don't suppose old King Jumbo ever had a tuxedo on in his life. We've done away with all the frills them old kings and potentates used to put on. Of course we've kept the best things—champagne and dancing girls and such. Ah that was the life! You know, Wilb, it's nice here, but sometime I kind of regret my splendid past."

"You may regret it worse before you're through," said Mr. Pope. "You've got us in a fine mess." And he told Ed about it.

"Why that's a darned shame!" said Ed. "Telling lies are they? No sense of reality, hey? What sense of reality has a dame got who don't see fun in fairy stories? Wilb, it makes my royal blood boil."

"I can hear it boiling," said Mr. Pope, "but it doesn't help the kids much. I'm kind of sick of your royal blood, Ed."

"It's good blood," said Ed. "We trace back direct to King Solomon. Hence my vaunted wisdom."

"Well you shift your vaunted wisdom into high," said Mr.

Pope, "and figure some way out. I'm in wrong as it is, for defending the children. I can't do anything."

"Wisdom seems to be in reverse at the moment," said Ed. "Now if I had a little drink—"

Mr. Pope went into the house and got a bottle. But several primings of Scotch seemed to have no effect on Ed's wisdom. It merely stimulated memories of his princely past, and brought to light details which would certainly have rendered him ineligible as a husband for any well brought up little girl. Mr. Pope who shared the bottle with him was so entertained by these intimate glimpses of court life that he presently forgot his problem, and merely sought to draw out further revelations. Until at last in addressing Ed as Your Highness, his tongue slipped on the fifth drink and he said, "But what did the Fifth Concubine do then, Your Harness?" They whooped over this so long and so loud that Mrs. Pope called from her window, "Wilbur is that you?" And with an admonition to Ed for God's sake think of something, Mr. Pope went back into the house.

Well it was the next evening that the children disappeared. When she went up to dress for dinner Mrs. Hubbard found a note from them. It said:

"Dear Mother: We are not liars. We are going away forever. We hope you won't feel bad. We hope you will be happy. Goodby forever.

Your loving ~~dauters~~ daugters
Jean and Silvie"

Mrs. Hubbard gave a loud scream, and everybody came running in, and she told them, and they about tore the house to pieces, but no children. No one had seen them for over an hour. Carrie the cook reported a large chocolate cake missing. And Mr. Pope went out to search the barn while they called the police.

"Hey, Ed," he said, "are the children out here?"

"I saw 'em making for the back gate with a chocolate cake about two hours ago," said Ed. "Why?" And when Mr. Pope told him he said, "O they won't get far. The state cops'll pick 'em up. Anyway they won't starve. Serves that Hubbard dame right, if you ask me."

"Well keep an eye out for 'em will you?" said Mr. Pope. "I've got to organize a search party."

So the cops came and everybody went out to comb the countryside except Mrs. Hubbard, who stayed on the porch, clasping and unclasping her hands and watching the driveway. But nothing moved in the driveway except the state cop who had been posted there. "O dear!" said Mrs. Hubbard, "O dear!"

And then a low voice in the shrubbery somewhere said, "If you want your children back, don't move or speak."

Mrs. Hubbard looked quickly around. The trooper was only a few yards down the drive. "Officer!" she yelled. "Quick! There's a man in the shrubbery. Get him!"

The trooper was quick all right. He drew his gun and dashed up past the porch into the garden. But in a minute he was back. "No one there, ma'am," he said.

"But I assure you there is," said Mrs. Hubbard. "He just spoke to me."

The cop looked puzzled. "It's all open on the other side," he said. "He couldn't hide. There's nothing there but Mr. Pope's horse. Hadn't I ought to tie him up?"

"No, no," said Mrs. Hubbard irritably. "Mr. Pope lets him roam around. I'm sure there's a man there."

So the cop went and looked again, and then without saying anything more went back to his post.

And in a minute the voice came again. "I told you not to speak," it said. "I'll give you one more chance. I'll bring the children to you on one condition."

"Are you a kidnaper?" whispered Mrs. Hubbard. "Do you want money? I'll arrange anything I can."

"No, ma'am," said the voice, "I ain't a kidnaper and I don't want money. If those kids come back it's up to them—not to me. I can bring 'em if I tell 'em you're sorry you said they were liars."

"Of course I'm sorry," said Mrs. Hubbard. "Poor little things. Although they did— How do *you* know about that?" she asked suddenly.

"We can't talk here," said the voice. "Go get that horse and lead him down to the barn. You can tell the cop what you're doing so he won't suspect anything."

So Mrs. Hubbard went and spoke to the trooper for a moment, and then went through the shrubbery to where Ed was standing, and led him into the barn. Ed clumped into his stall, and as she stood hesitating by the door the voice spoke again.

"Here's my condition," it said. "You'll tell 'em you're sorry, and you'll tell 'em they can go to their Aunt Caroline's. And *then* you'll tell 'em a fairy story."

"All—all right," said Mrs. Hubbard humbly. "I promise."

"Come along, kids," said the voice.

There was a giggle and a rush, and Jean and Silvie tumbled down the stairs from the loft into their mother's arms.

"O darlings," said Mrs. Hubbard, "where *have* you been?"

"We aren't liars, are we, mother?" said Jean, and Silvie said, "We ran away with Prince Ed."

"O children," said Mrs. Hubbard, "I'm sorry I said you were liars, and you *can* go to your Aunt Caroline's, but I do wish you wouldn't make up—"

"Careful!" said the voice. "There was a third condition."

"O yes, mother," said Jean, "you were going to tell us a story."

"But we must go into the house first, dears," said Mrs. Hubbard, "and let people know—"

"Tell it now," said the voice.

"O dear!" said Mrs. Hubbard helplessly. "Well—once upon a time there was a—a house named Edgar."

"Houses don't have names, mother," said Silvie.

"This one did," said Mrs. Hubbard desperately. "He was a small house, and he had one wing containing two bedrooms."

"Who lived in him?" said Jean.

"A little girl named Mollie Wink, and her Aunt Martha," said Mrs. Hubbard.

"If he had a wing maybe he could fly," said Silvie.

"That's just what he'd always wanted to do," said Mrs. Hubbard, "but of course with only one wing, he couldn't. He thought if he had two wings he would like to try it. So he tried to get Aunt Martha to build another one. He squeezed up all of his rooms as small as he could, and one day Aunt Martha said, 'Mollie, we don't seem to have as much room here as we used to. I guess we'll have to build on another wing.' So she did. And the night the new wing was completed, Edgar waited until Mollie and Aunt Martha were asleep—"

Just then a light was flashed in their eyes, and the trooper's voice said, "Hey, what goes on here? Why you've found 'em!"

"O thank goodness!" said Mrs. Hubbard, turning toward the door. "I hoped you'd come. There's a man in here, officer—the man that took the children." And she pushed the little girls before her out of the barn.

The trooper drew his gun and stood in the doorway.

"Come on," he said. "Come out or I'll shoot."

"Better not, copper," said the voice. "You might hit the horse."

The trooper hesitated a minute, and then went into the barn. He found the button and turned on the electric light. But there was nobody there except Ed.

"There's no other door," said Mrs. Hubbard. "He must still be here."

"Maybe gone up into the loft," said the trooper, and went upstairs. Mrs. Hubbard stood outside and watched the door. She could hear the trooper rummaging around, and then there was a loud laugh and immediately he came thumping down again.

"Who was that laughed?" he said.

"I thought it was you," said Mrs. Hubbard.

"It was downstairs," said the trooper, "but there's nobody here now."

"Nobody came out," said Mrs. Hubbard.

"It was Prince Ed, mother," said Silvie, and the two little girls laughed heartily.

"Well this beats me," said the trooper, coming to the door. "Nobody's gone in and nobody's come out, and still there's somebody here." He looked suspiciously at Mrs. Hubbard. "Who's this Prince Ed?"

"O it's just a fairy story character the children invented," said Mrs. Hubbard.

"It's the horse," said Jean. "He talks."

The cop grunted and then as lights and voices came around the corner of the house, he said, "Here they come back. You better take the kids in the house, ma'am. We'll find him if he's here."

Well of course they didn't find him, and as the troopers began to suspect a hoax, they didn't try very hard. When they had gone the Popes and the Hubbards talked it over.

"I can't make it out," said Mrs. Hubbard. "The children say they were in the loft all the time, but you searched the barn, Wilbur."

"Well, I—yes I did," said Mr. Pope hastily. "What explanation do they give?"

"O some nonsense about that horse of yours having hidden them and talked to me," said Mrs. Hubbard.

"There must be some logical explanation," said Mr. Hubbard. "Someone certainly talked to Margie and he was there—in a barn with only one door. And yet nobody could find him."

"Well," said Mr. Pope, "the children's explanation may be incredible, but it's the only logical one I've heard offered. Have you a better one, Margie?"

"Don't be ridiculous, Wilbur," said Mrs. Pope.

"I've heard some talk," said Mr. Pope, "about a sense of reality, and not knowing truth from fiction. Seriously, Margie, do you think your story is any more credible than the children's?"

"Really, Wilbur," began Mr. Hubbard, but Mrs. Hubbard, who had turned white, said, "I'm afraid he's right, George. I just don't—I can't—" She stopped. "I think I'd better go see if the children want anything," she said.

The others just sat and looked blankly at one another. Then Mr. Pope got up and went out. In the hall he stopped. Upstairs Mrs. Hubbard's voice was saying, "So when Aunt Martha woke up that morning and looked out of the window she saw nothing but clouds. 'My gracious,' she said, 'whatever has become of our hen-coop?' And then she looked down and—and—"

"O go on, mother," said Silvie. "Why didn't you ever tell us this story before?"

"Do you like it, darlings?" said Mrs. Hubbard. Her voice sounded a little hesitant but very happy. Mr. Pope grinned and went out to the barn.

"Hi, Wilb," said Ed. "Well I fixed it all right."

"You did at that," said Mr. Pope. "Your royal sire'd be proud of you. There's just one thing though. What became of the chocolate cake?"

"Well I'll tell you," said Ed. "I was afraid those kids would make themselves sick. I thought and thought, Wilb, how to get 'em to give it up. And then I thought of the diamond coach drawn by six milk-white woodchucks that my grandfather old Hoopla XIV used to ride around in. It pretty near broke my heart to part with it because it's an heirloom, besides being darn near unique. But I said to myself—"

"All right, all right," interrupted Mr. Pope. "So you traded it for the cake. And when do they get delivery on it?"

"When they're eighteen," said Ed.

"Pretty small business, I call it," said Mr. Pope and Ed said, "Well what would you have done?"

"I'd have saved a piece for me," said Mr. Pope.

"Pooh!" said Ed, "it wasn't very good anyway. Look, Wilb, did I ever tell you about the time old Hoopla's harem went on a sit-down strike?"

Ed Quenches an Old Flame

Wilbur Pope's wife, Carlotta, was always a sort of storm center. I guess it was because she was so beautiful. I guess men that want quiet lives ought to marry homely women. Mr. Pope sometimes wished that his wife was the kind of woman to whom her husband says, "You will always be beautiful to me, dear." But she wasn't, and he just had to put up with it.

There was this Jed Witherspoon, for instance. Mr. Pope did not exactly dislike Mr. Witherspoon but if Mr. Witherspoon had fallen down an elevator shaft or off a reasonably tall building Mr. Pope would not have gone mad with grief. For once, before Mrs. Pope had been Mrs. Pope, Mr. Witherspoon had been engaged to her. Of course the engagement had been broken but Mr. Witherspoon considered this, and her subsequent marriage to Mr. Pope, as merely a temporary check to his plans. And although he was only one of a large crowd of admirers who dropped in weekends at the Pope house in Mt. Kisco, he was the most annoying to Mr. Pope. For he looked indulgently on Mr. Pope and the status quo, while his manner to Mrs. Pope was decidedly proprietary. He was quite open about his bland confidence that time would adjust affairs in his favor.

Well, after a year or two during which Mr. Witherspoon had M.C.'d practically all social activities in the Pope home, Mr. Pope began to worry. Such assurance, he felt, must be based on something more substantial than conceit. And at last he spoke to Mrs. Pope about it.

Mrs. Pope just thought he was funny, and when he insisted she got cross. Being one-eighth Spanish she got cross one-eighth quicker than other women and that is pretty quick. "Don't be ridiculous," she said. "If I'd wanted Jed I would have married him in the first place."

"I'm not asking what you would have done," said Mr. Pope. "I'm asking what you intend."

"Well Wilb, how was it?" "Horrible," said Wilbur.

"Goodness, the heavy father!" Mrs. Pope burst into laughter which was pretty but ominous. "What are your intentions, madam, with regard to my little Jed? How he would laugh!"

"That makes two of you," Mr. Pope said. "But you still don't answer. I want to know."

"There isn't anything to know," said Mrs. Pope. "Don't be idiotic."

So Mr. Pope went on worrying.

Well, Mr. Pope was commuting peacefully homeward on the 5:28 one evening when Mr. Witherspoon sat down beside him.

"Hello, Wilbur," said Mr. Witherspoon, and then he sighed heavily and said, "Why, oh why do we do it?"

"Do what?" said Mr. Pope, and Mr. Witherspoon said, "Spend half our lives on trains, looking at the same grimy scenery, reading the same grimy papers. And for what?"

"Space," said Mr. Pope vaguely. "Air, grass, the foot on the clean turf and the eyes on the clouds."

"Give me the foot on the rail and the head in the clouds," said Mr. Witherspoon. "No, these fellows that live in town have the best of it. If they want the country, they can always go out and visit friends weekends."

"They can and do," said Mr. Pope bitterly.

"Seriously," Mr. Witherspoon said, "haven't you and Carlotta ever thought of taking an apartment in town for the winter? If my sister only liked New York better I'd take one tomorrow. But even though we've been practically pushed into the attic, now that Bess and her children have come to live with us, she won't consider it."

"As a matter of fact," said Mr. Pope, "we have talked of taking an apartment. But we couldn't afford to unless we could rent the Mt. Kisco house. And there's not much chance of that."

"Well, I don't know," said Mr. Witherspoon thoughtfully. "Grace and I—" He looked up quickly. "You know we've been looking for a house since Bess got here," he said. "The children get on Grace's nerves, and we thought that if just during the winter—"

"I see," said Mr. Pope. "H'm. There's Ed to consider—"

"Oh, the horse could stay right in your stable," said Mr. Witherspoon. "Your man could continue to look after him, and if you wanted to exercise him, we'd be only too glad to have you and Carlotta come out any weekend, you know."

Mr. Pope wriggled uncomfortably. "Well, Jed," he said, "I

can talk it over with Carlotta. Frankly, I hadn't thought very seriously about it."

"Oh, it will be all right with Carlotta," said Mr. Witherspoon.

"You've spoken to her about it?" said Mr. Pope, and Mr. Witherspoon admitted that he had sounded her out on the subject.

Mr. Pope grunted. "Well," he said, "I'll talk to her tonight."

So he did. He didn't talk very long.

"I don't see why you're so contrary, Wilbur," she said. "You've always agreed with me about an apartment, and then when we get this heaven-sent opportunity you don't want to take it."

"Sure, I agreed with you," said Mr. Pope. "I didn't think you'd ever dig up a tenant."

After that of course he didn't have a leg to stand on, and he abandoned the argument and went out to see Ed.

Ed had the vocabulary of a taxi driver, which was only natural since he claimed to have spent part of his youth in the hacking business. And he certainly talked that evening, when Mr. Pope told him about moving to the city.

"I never would have believed it of you, Wilb, never," he said. "I thought you and me'd agreed we had just the life we liked, ridin' around over the hills and shootin' the breeze and droppin' in at Barney's for a beer. And now, just because you got a middle-aged urge to go sportin' around in night clubs, you'd leave me out here alone all winter. Why, you're the darnedest meanest guy in Westchester County."

"Nonsense!" said Mr. Pope. "I'll come out and ride every weekend I can. And you'll be comfortable. John'll look after you, and I'll see he gives you your quota of beer."

"Got it all worked out, ain't you?" said Ed. "Say! Is there a woman back of this?"

"Sure. Carlotta's back of it. Look, Ed, I don't like it any more than you do, but there's no way out."

"I can see six ways out from here," said Ed, "but not for a guy that says, 'Yes, ma'am' every time his wife flickers an eyelid at him."

"I won't have you talk about Carlotta, Ed," said Mr. Pope coldly.

"I ain't talkin' about her," said the horse. "I'm talkin' about you. I don't say I like your wife, but I got a lot of respect for her. She gets what she wants. Now if you just put your foot down about this, hard enough to make her teeth jingle, she'll forget all about any apartment and snuggle down here as quiet as a moth in a blanket."

"You're the one that had better snuggle down quiet and happy," said Mr. Pope. "Because that's how it's got to be."

So Ed didn't say any more then. A week later the Popes moved into an apartment on East 65th Street—which, it turned out, Mrs. Pope had already selected—and the Witherspoons moved into the Pope house.

The first few days weren't so bad, and Mr. Pope discovered a number of advantages in living in town. The only annoyance was Mr. Witherspoon, who dropped in every afternoon on his way—as he said—to Grand Central. Though Mr. Pope failed to see why he should leave the office at two-thirty to catch a six-thirty train. "I thought we came to town for a change," he said. "With Jed around all the time it's just like home."

"Oh, pooh," said Mrs. Pope. "He's just trying to be decent. He just wants to assure us that everything is all right out there."

But one afternoon he came home and found Miss Witherspoon there.

Miss Witherspoon was older than her brother, a small woman who might have been rather pretty if she hadn't had such large ears. As it was, you were so conscious of her ears that you never got around to her other features.

"Why, hello, Grace," said Mr. Pope. "What brings you into town?"

"A rather unpleasant errand," said Miss Witherspoon, and Mrs. Pope said, "Grace says our house is haunted."

"I didn't say that," retorted Miss Witherspoon. "I said it *appeared* to be haunted. I do not believe in supernatural manifestations. Wilbur, you didn't particularly want to rent us the house, did you?"

"Frankly, no," said Mr. Pope. "But Carlotta—"

"Exactly," said Miss Witherspoon. "I understood from Jed that that was the situation. But I didn't suppose that, having made your bargain, you would try to get out of it."

"Oh come, Grace," put in Mrs. Pope, "you surely don't suggest that Wilbur has been playing those tricks? Why, he—he isn't qualified to haunt a house. Anyway, why hasn't Jed said anything about it when I've seen him?"

"He didn't want to worry you. But when it got so bad—"

"Suppose you tell me just what has been going on," Mr. Pope said.

"There have been a number of things," said Miss Witherspoon. "Noises at night, and tappings on windows, and—disturbances. But the principal thing is that all the lights in the house suddenly go out, and then there's this screeching. Or a sort of maniac laughter."

"How often has this happened?"

"Five or six times."

"Where did the screeching come from?"

"It seemed to be either in, or just outside the house."

"Well, I don't know," said Mr. Pope. "We've never heard anything of the kind ourselves, but the likeliest explanation is a couple of local drunks on the road. As to the direction the yells came from, I think your ears may well have deceived you—" He stopped abruptly, with the horrified realization that he probably couldn't have thought up a more insulting remark if he'd tried.

"I doubt if we are getting anywhere," said Miss Witherspoon stiffly, "but I should like to ask how your local drunks account for the lights? We had an electrician out, and he went over the wiring and reported everything in order. The only way he could account for it was that somebody was getting at the fuse box, which as you know is in the stable. But we locked the stable door, and it still continues."

"H'm," said Mr. Pope, "the—ah, the stable door, yes. And of course, Ed—" He pulled himself together. "Well, Grace," he said, "all I can say is, if you want to give up the house, we'll release you."

"I'm sure you would," she said acidly. "But we do not intend to give up the house. I'm going to find out what's behind all this. And if it's some scheme of yours for getting rid of us—"

"Really, Grace," said Mrs. Pope, "that sort of accusation is rather silly. We're as much in the dark as you are."

"We have been in the dark most of the time since we took the house," said Miss Witherspoon. "However, Jed was sure you had nothing to do with it, Carlotta, and he thought the best thing might be for you both to come out next weekend, and we could look into it together."

"Pleasant weekend for me," said Mr. Pope, "with everyone expecting me to burst into ghoulish yowls any minute."

After Miss Witherspoon had gone the Popes had an acrid row. Mrs. Pope accused Mr. Pope of trying to drive the

Witherspoons away, so that he would have an excuse for going back to Mt. Kisco. Nothing would persuade her that he was not manifesting in some obscure way—perhaps through old John.

The only thing for Mr. Pope to do was to go out and investigate, so on Friday they took the train for Mt. Kisco. From the first Mr. Pope found Mr. Witherspoon's attitude very trying. Mr. Witherspoon took it as a simple matter of fact that Mr. Pope was causing the trouble, which he affected to find rather entertaining. "There's always been a ghostlike quality about you, Wilbur," he said. "You've never fully materialized for me somehow. It seems quite natural that you should continue to haunt this house. When Carlotta gets her divorce," he went on, "I'm sure it will be on the grounds of inhuman and supernatural behavior."

"It pleases me that you envy me my spiritual qualities," said Mr. Pope. "It shows a certain blind groping upward from the sub-human level."

Mrs. Pope surprised Mr. Pope by giggling at this. It made him feel a little better, but not much. He went to see Ed.

The horse greeted him grumpily. "What's the idea," he demanded, "leaving me here alone for three weeks with nobody to talk to? I could have died, and you wouldn't have cared."

"I wouldn't specially, at that," said Mr. Pope. "Haunting a house is excusable when you're dead. When you're still alive, it's indecent."

"It may be," said Ed, "but it's a hell of a lot of fun. That is—I assume you refer to the recent local disturbances. Funny thing, Wilb, there was never anything queer about this house before, was there?"

"Nothing I couldn't explain," said Mr. Pope. "Of course there's nothing I can't explain now, either."

"You'd better explain right away to that Witherspoon dame, then," said Ed. "She was all for leaving last week, but her brother wouldn't let her. He said it wouldn't be fair to your wife. I suppose you know that it was your wife that engineered this whole scheme? Miss Witherspoon wanted to take an apartment in New York, but your wife and that Jed talked her out of it."

"Nonsense," said Mr. Pope. "Grace doesn't like the city; Jed told me that himself."

"Yeah? Don't be a sucker, Wilb. Jed was looking for an apartment until your wife told him she wanted to go into

town for the winter herself, but couldn't get a tenant for
this house. He's kind of anxious to please your wife—or
didn't you know about that? So the two of them high-
pressured Grace into giving up the town idea. I heard the
whole blame thing when Jed and Grace were showin' their
teeth at each other about it the other night on the terrace.
They'd had kind of a full evening, and I guess they was
pretty wrought up; the ghost had dropped by and there was
some goblins being ghastly out in the shrubbery. Grace said
she was fed up and was going in town to a hotel till she
found an apartment. Jed says she can't do that. 'It wouldn't
be fair to Carlotta,' he says. 'All this monkey business is
only that thick-witted dog in the manger, Wilbur,' he says
—well, I'm just repeatin' his words. And not all of 'em either.
He had a lot to say about how mean you was to your wife,
and how she hated it in the country. They agreed you was
pretty generally a prize rat. And then Grace come around and
said she'd stick a while longer. 'Only,' she says, 'if Wilbur
don't stop this ghost business I'm going to appeal to the
police.' So you see, Wilb, your wife—"

"I see you're leading the conversation as far as possible
from your own ghostly activities," said Mr. Pope. "And I
won't have you criticizing Carlotta."

"I ain't saying anything against her," replied Ed. "Only—
well, ain't this Jed kind of sweet on her?"

"I don't suppose he comes around primarily to see me,"
said Mr. Pope. "But that's true of a number of my friends.
What of it?"

"There's this of it. He figures he's getting the inside track.
He sees more of her in the city than he did out here. And at
the same time he gets her the place she wants to live in. And
folks know about this deal, and they're talking. And—well,
your wife should be like whosit's—Potiphar's wife. Beyond
reproach—"

"Caesar's, you dope," said Mr. Pope.

"Yeah," said Ed. "Well, it was a long time ago, anyway.
Just the same—"

"Let's get back to the hauntings," said Mr. Pope. He
went over to the fuse box and opened it. "Sure, you could
unscrew a fuse with your teeth all right. Then go to the window and yell—"

"Not yell," said Ed reproachfully. "No, that's kid stuff.
You'd never get anywhere haunting a house, Wilb. You got
to have an artistic nature, I guess. You don't want to shatter

their nerves; you want to make 'em kind of curdle. I give
'em a low giggle. When you're alone in the dark, there ain't
anything more horrible than a low obscene giggle comin'
maybe from a chair that you know there ain't anybody sitting in. And sometimes I vary it. I got a loathsome chuckle,
Wilb, that—"

"Sure," interrupted Mr. Pope. "Well, you're going to lay
off your loathsome chucklings. These people have rented the
house, and I'm going to see that they enjoy it in peace.
Besides, you're making a monkey of me. They all suspect
me."

"Let's not go into who's making a monkey of you," said
Ed. "Oh gosh, Wilb, this ghost stuff is the only fun I have.
They lock the stable every night so nobody can get at the
fuse box. I haven't been out for an evening in two weeks."

"I'll fix that for you," said Mr. Pope. "But this haunting
has got to stop now."

"Okay," said Ed. "But look, Wilb. Let me put on my act,
while you're here—"

"No!" said Mr. Pope shortly. "But hold on," he said.
"Maybe it's all right, at that. It would prove I have no connection, wouldn't it? All right, just once then."

At half-past nine, when they were starting their second
rubber of bridge, the lights all went out.

Miss Witherspoon gave a sort of shuddering moan, but
Mr. Witherspoon said sharply, "Don't be silly, Grace. I told
you Wilbur would arrange something for tonight, just so
it would appear that he has nothing to do with it. He doesn't
think we're bright enough to guess that he might have an
accomplice." He got up and lit a candle. "There's always
this pause before anything else happens. Rather a subtle
touch, Wilbur. I wouldn't have thought it of you."

Then, from out of the night, through the open window,
there came a high inhuman giggle. Mrs. Pope gave a squeal
of fright, but Miss Witherspoon jumped up, overturning the
card table. "I won't stay in this house another night!" she exclaimed in a tremulous voice. "I don't care if it is a hoax.
It's too awful! It's—oh!" She dropped back into her chair and
covered her face. For outside in the darkness something
gave a gross oily chuckle.

It was loathsome. Mr. Pope told himself it was only Ed.
But his skin crawled. Then he pulled himself together.

He got up. "Well, Jed, what are we waiting for? I thought
you asked us out here to investigate?"

But Mr. Witherspoon seemed shaken. "What is there to investigate? If you think I'm going to stumble around to find out something you already know—"

"Oh, go on, Jed," interrupted Mrs. Pope. And Mr. Pope said, "In other words, you aren't really sure I'm the ghost after all?"

"I'll go with you," said Miss Witherspoon suddenly. "Anything is better than sitting here, waiting."

They started toward the hall and the others trailed after them.

But as they reached the hall the lights suddenly went on again, and at the same moment the doorbell rang.

For a moment they just looked at one another. Then Mr. Pope said, "Your honor, Jed. I'm only a guest here. It's probably some horrid grisly spectre, squatting out there. There must be something pretty hellish in your past, to account for all this."

Mr. Witherspoon hung back. Mrs. Pope pushed him aside and opened the door.

"Well, well," said Mr. Pope. "The inspector, not the spectre. Hello, Tom."

The state trooper touched his cap. "How do you do, Mrs. Pope." Then, looking over her shoulder: "Evening, Mr. Witherspoon. Anything wrong here? I saw your lights were out again and—"

"Oh, officer, I'm glad you're here," said Miss Witherspoon. "Yes, it's the same disturbance again. We were just going out to investigate. Though I imagine," she added venomously, "if you question Mr. Pope, you'll find out more than any investigation of ours will produce."

The trooper looked reproachfully at Mr. Pope. "You hadn't ought to do it, Mr. Pope," he said. "You could get in a lot of trouble."

"If you'll explain to me how I can produce these effects when I'm in the city," Mr. Pope began, but Mr. Witherspoon interrupted him. "You weren't in the city tonight. And even when you're presumably in the city—well, Carlotta says you've spent a lot of evenings at the office."

"Well, let's have a look," said the trooper. They all went out to the stable.

"The door's open," said Mr. Witherspoon. "And your horse isn't here."

"I leave it that way in the summer, so Ed can have the run of the lot next door," said Mr. Pope. "He's probably

gone out there now. I left it open when I went out to talk to—
that is—er—to—"

"To talk to whom, Wilbur?" snapped Miss Witherspoon.

Mr. Pope endeavored to rationalize his slip, but it had
been fatal. Nobody believed him. It was plain that he had
been giving instructions to some confederate, and the stable
was thoroughly searched. But though much dust and evidences of mice were stirred up and sneezed at, when the
trooper finally emerged, festooned with cobwebs, he had
nothing incriminatory to report.

As they started back to the house, however, the atmosphere of suspicion was so oppressive that Mr. Pope stopped.
"I'm going to get Ed," he said. "Perhaps I'll saddle him and
take a ride. You can discuss my crimes more freely, I imagine,
in my absence." And he turned toward the hedge which
separated his lawn from the adjoining field.

"Well, Wilb, how was it?" the horse asked.

"Horrible," said Mr. Pope. "I don't know that I ever
heard anything so utterly base." He led Ed back to the
stable and got a bottle of Scotch from the harness closet.
"Unfortunately, it didn't prove anything. Even Carlotta is
sure now that I'm working with an accomplice, and that I
produced the chuckle by ventriloquism or something. They're
up there discussing me now." He took a drink and passed the
bottle. "I needed that! Heavens, Ed, there are certainly
depths of vileness in your soul that are better left un-
plumbed."

"Yeah?" said Ed. "That shows how much you know about
the histrionic art. I borrowed that chuckle from old man
Harkness that owned the livery stable. If you want to plumb
some depths, get him to reminiscin'. Side of him, I'm a
little friskin' lamb. But if you have a natural talent for
acting, like I got, it ain't necessary for you to go out and
knock off your old man in order to play Hamlet."

"It would be a great privilege to see you as Hamlet," said
Mr. Pope. "You'd have them writhing in the aisles."

"Yeah? You laugh, but listen to this." Ed leaned against
the wall in a meditative attitude, with one foreleg crossed
over the other, and began. "To be or not to be, that is the
question. Whether to—to—" He stopped, cleared his throat,
then again gave that coarse chuckle. "Sorry, Wilb," he said,
"I ain't letter perfect and that's a fact. And when I get
stuck, old man Harkness seems to creep in somehow."

"It's hard to shift from one role to another so suddenly," said Mr. Pope. "Particularly when the first one is so sympathetic to you."

"Well, I did like the old stinker," said Ed. "He'd sit there all day long, chucklin' over his iniquities. Like this." And the horse chuckled again.

And at that moment the trooper, followed by the Witherspoons and Mrs. Pope, burst into the stable.

"You heard it, officer!" exclaimed Miss Witherspoon. "That's why I made you come out and listen."

"Wilbur!" exclaimed Mrs. Pope. "It was really you all the time!" He noticed with some bewilderment that she didn't look as mad as she ought to be.

"I demand that you arrest him!" said Miss Witherspoon furiously. "Such actions—why, they're insanity!"

"Well now, ma'am," cut in the trooper, "let's go up to the house and talk this over quietly. Of course he was making the noise; there's no one else here. But—"

"What's all the row?" demanded Mr. Pope. "If you're going to try to get every man that talks to his horse or dog certified insane, this whole county will be just one big asylum."

The trooper shook his head. "That isn't good enough, Mr. Pope. The evidence is all against you. Now look, as I get it, you want to get these folks out of your house; that's why you're playing these tricks. Well, they can cause quite a lot of trouble for you—malicious mischief, and so on. Why don't you give 'em your word that you'll lay off the ghost stuff? It ain't very dignified anyway. And I think Mr. Witherspoon would drop any charges—"

"But I keep telling you," said Mr. Pope angrily, "that I have nothing to do with these noises!"

They had moved outside the stable and were standing grouped by the door. Mrs. Pope put her hand on her husband's arm. "Wilbur, please!" Then she turned to Mr. Witherspoon. "Jed, don't let's have a scandal about this thing."

Mr. Witherspoon took her arm and drew her away from Mr. Pope. "I'm sorry, Carlotta, but the lease is in Grace's name. And really," he said solemnly, "I'm afraid that Wilbur is—" He shook his head. "At first I thought he was jealous. I've seen you quite often in town. But tonight—"

She shook him off. "Don't talk like a fool!" she said. And Mr. Pope gaped at her. At various times similar words had been directed at him, but never with such a bite of contempt.

"But, Carlotta," Mr. Witherspoon began, and stopped; for from inside the barn came again that depraved chuckle.

"Oh, my lord!" quavered Mr. Witherspoon, and the beam of the trooper's flashlight shot out and swept over roof and walls, then probed the dusty interior. Quite plainly nothing human could have made a sound. And Miss Witherspoon turned and ran for the house.

The chuckle came again, and Ed added a further refinement of horror, for he threw up his head, snorted, and then, with a shrill neigh, came charging into the open, his eyes rolling with terror.

The trooper snapped off the light and backed away from the door. "I guess this is out of my line, Mr. Witherspoon," he said. "What you want is a priest." And he followed Miss Witherspoon.

Mr. Pope took his wife's arm and led her up toward the house. "Better come, Jed," he said. "The goblins'll get you."

Mr. Witherspoon hesitated. "You've got a confederate in that stable somewhere," he said determinedly, "and by gosh, I'm going to find him." He turned back and switched on the stable light. Mr. Pope shrugged and went on.

"Wilbur," said Mrs. Pope, "what *is* causing all this? I don't—I never believed in such things, but if it's really . . . Oh, come clean, can't you?"

"What does it matter?" he said. "You don't want to live in the house anyway."

"Who said I didn't? I'm not so crazy about town. It's not —well . . ."

Mr. Pope was pretty astonished. But this particular subject had better wait, he thought. He said, "Probably some defect in the wiring. I mean these lights going out—not you."

"But those dreadful noises?"

Mr. Pope thought fast. What could chuckle—an infected brook, a corrupt squirrel? Then he remembered a line of poetry that had stuck in his mind because of its odd sound. "Yaffles, on a chuckle, skim, low to laugh—" and so on.

"Did you ever hear of the yaffle?" he asked. "It's an English bird. A night bird, and it chuckles. Well, somebody brought a pair over a few years ago, and they're becoming domesticated. That was what we heard, I'm quite sure."

"In the stable?"

"I believe they nest in stables."

"How clever of you, darling," said Mrs. Pope sarcastically.

"Isn't it!" he said airily. And at that minute the lights all went out.

"That nice yaffle!" said Mrs. Pope, and immediately the yaffle spoke again from the stable—an eerie chuckle.

But this time the chuckle was followed by confused sounds —scramblings, thumpings, and then a loud scream. And Jed came pounding across the lawn and flung himself into Mr. Pope's arms.

"Wilbur! That thing—it isn't human! It attacked me! For God's sake, get into the house!"

They supported Mr. Witherspoon into the living room, where a candle was still burning, and eased him into a chair. The shoulder of his coat was torn out.

"Take it easy, Jed," said Mr. Pope. "Papa fix. What's it all about?"

"I was in the barn," Mr. Witherspoon gasped. "At the far end. Looking around. Then the lights went out. I could just see where the door was, and started toward it, when I heard that beastly noise again and something huge blotted out the doorway. It came toward me, sort of tramping, and making those awful chucklings. So I tried to duck past it. Then it attacked me." He leaned back, shuddering. "I tell you the thing's a monster of some kind. A huge thing like a gorilla, with long shaggy hair, and huge jaws. I could hear them snapping at me."

"Oh, but really, Jed," said Mrs. Pope.

"Look," said Mr. Witherspoon, and held out his hand. In it were clutched a dozen or more coarse black hairs. "I grabbed at the thing and got these. And the awful part was that it spoke!"

"You mean," said Mrs. Pope, "that it was a man, dressed up?"

"No man could be as huge as that," said Mr. Witherspoon. "Where's Grace? We're getting out of here right now!"

"I'm here," said Miss Witherspoon from the doorway. "Yes, Jed, we're leaving. I've packed, and I've called a cab. I admit, Wilbur, that there doesn't seem to be any hoax on your part. But I can't absolve either you or Carlotta. You must have known when we rented the place— Oh, there come the lights!"

"What did the—er—monster say to you, Jed?" Mr. Pope asked.

"You think it's very funny, don't you?" said Mr. Wither-

spoon. "Well, all I can say is, you go out to the barn yourself and see what you get. I've heard foul language in my
time, but this—oh, it doesn't bear thinking of." He got up.

"One minute," said Mr. Pope. "I have a suggestion. We
now have an apartment in town which we don't want to keep.
And you have this house ditto. Now my suggestion is that
we just exchange. Carlotta and I will stay here tonight, and
I'll pick up our stuff in town in the morning. Think it over.
I'll be back in a minute." And he went out to the stable.

"Hi, Wilb," said Ed. "How was that for timing?"

"It was perfect," said Mr. Pope. "But what on earth did
you say to Jed?"

" 'Twas something old man Harkness said to Jasper Bowers
when he give him one of them exploding cigars."

"But what was it?"

"I don't know as I care to soil my lips with it," said Ed
virtuously. "Not unless I could wash my mouth out after-
wards with something good and strong."

"Okay," said Mr. Pope, and went over to the harness
closet.

So Ed told him.

After the second drink Mr. Pope had revived sufficiently
to speak. "Well," he said, "I'd say you'd done enough
without beating the poor chap up."

"You don't know how to treat such guys," said Ed. "Instead of taking a crack at him you take a wisecrack at him.
That ain't the way to treat that baby."

"Well," said Mr. Pope, "I've got to get back to say good-
bye. Let me have a few hairs out of your mane, will you?"

"Jed want 'em for a keepsake?" said Ed. "Okay. No, leave
the bottle. I guess I earned it."

Back in the house the Witherspoons were just coming
downstairs with their bags. Mr. Pope held out the hairs
from Ed's mane to Mr. Witherspoon. "Had a tussle with the
monster myself. Just compare these hairs with yours, Jed."

Mr. Witherspoon stared at them. "You mean that y-you—"

"They're out of Ed's mane," said Mr. Pope. "Poor Ed! He's
jittery from having been attacked like that in the dark."

"Nonsense," said Mr. Witherspoon. "I told you that the
thing spoke!"

"Figment of your imagination," said Mr. Pope. "Projection
of your fears. Welling up from the sinks of your subconscious."

Mrs. Pope's clear high laugh interrupted him. "Oh, Jed, you'll be the death of me!"

Mr. Witherspoon looked at her, then turned. "Come, Grace. There's the taxi."

"And now," said Mr. Pope, "just how fond are you of Jed? And no more stalling, Carlotta."

"You didn't think I was *really* fond of him, did you?" She smiled faintly.

"Yes. He's made himself ridiculous tonight, so you're rather off him. But—"

"Oh, stop it, Wilbur!" She caught his arm. "Why, how could you ever think—"

"How could I ever think anything else?" he demanded. "You would never say anything. The trouble with you, Carlotta, is that you're one of those women who keep all their emotions but anger under pretty good control. So no one ever—"

"Do I indeed?" said Mrs. Pope demurely, and threw her arms around him."

"Well," said Mr. Pope presently, "not always."

Medium Rare

I guess this Ed of Wilbur Pope's was more patriotic than most horses are. I don't mean to say that horses as a class aren't patriotic, but I never knew any other horses that talked about it. Of course Ed wouldn't talk to anybody but Mr. Pope, but he felt pretty strongly about America, and I guess that was why he got so excited about trying to capture this spy.

On several of their Sunday rambles over the pleasant Westchester landscape, Ed and Mr. Pope had noticed this man. He was middle-aged, short and bearded, always had field glasses and a camera strapped to him, and seemed to haunt the vicinity of the reservoir or the big dam. He popped in and out of the woods, appeared and vanished like an active and rather distinguished-looking gnome. He limped with his left leg.

Ed was all ready to order out the firing squad the second time they saw him. Mr. Pope just laughed. "You're letting your imagination run away with you," he said. "Oh, sure, he acts queer. That's just the trouble. He acts too much like a saboteur to really be one."

Ed snorted. "Never heard such tripe in my life! He acts like a spy, so he can't be one! I suppose I look like a horse, so I'm probably a camel!"

"Some people have expressed that opinion," murmured Mr. Pope, and a moment later found himself sitting in the road while Ed clumped off toward home. He had to call several times, and then apologize at the top of his lungs before Ed finally consented to overlook the insult and return.

As Mr. Pope was brushing himself off, the alleged spy suddenly appeared again from a thick planting of young pines beside the road and came toward him. "Can I help you, sir? Are you hurt?"

"Oh, thank you—no," Mr. Pope said. "My horse is a bit skittish at times, but—" It suddenly occurred to him that the

The trooper fired as Ed sailed over the hedge.
"That fellow means business!" he told Mr. Pope.

man must have thought the whole incident rather queer. "I suppose you heard me apologizing to him," he said with a laugh. "Well, you see—I kicked him, and quite naturally he threw me off. Under the circumstances—well, why shouldn't one apologize to an animal? After all, they have feelings—"

"Of course. I quite understand," the man said. "I often find myself talking to the birds. I'm interested in them, you see—making a census of the migrant birds in this part of the state. Hence these." He indicated the camera and glasses. "My name is Smith—Professor John Smith, of, er—Columbia." Then, without waiting for Mr. Pope to reply, he said, "Well, good afternoon, sir," and disappeared into the pines.

Ed and Mr. Pope rode on for a time in silence. Then Ed exclaimed suddenly: "See how scared he acted, and how he ducked out!"

"Nonsense!" Mr. Pope said. "I tell you, no trained saboteur would act as suspicious as that."

"All right, all right!" Ed said crossly. "But if that guy's John Smith, then I'm Pocahontas."

Mr. Pope dismissed Professor Smith from his mind, but Ed decided to go in for a little counter-espionage. He was never locked up at night, and so was free to wander as he pleased. So he spent several nights investigating. And the following Saturday as they were starting out for a ride he said, "Say, Wilb, you know that place on the road that goes up by the reservoir where we saw that guy said his name was Smith last week? Well, just beyond, there's a little dirt road goes up into the hills. He lives up there."

Mr. Pope said all right, and what of it?

"It's just this of it," Ed said. "Maybe the guy's name is Smith, and maybe he's as innocent as a new-laid egg. But if so, maybe you can tell me why twice this last week there's a swell-looking blonde baby drives up and goes into the house with a lot of packages, and then comes out after an hour or so and creeps off down the hill without even switching on the lights?"

Mr. Pope grinned. "Good lord, Ed, you must have been brought up in a young ladies' seminary!"

"Oh, is that so? Well, I guess I'd ha' spotted anything lovey-dovey, as quick as the next one. No, sir, sex don't rear its ugly head in this nohow. And what do you make of it, Wilb?"

Mr. Pope didn't make anything of it, and didn't want to. He refused to argue and suggested beer.

So after they had dropped in at Barney's and put down a couple of bottles, they went up on one of the hills overlooking the reservoir, and there they saw Professor Smith again. He was standing on a little open knoll and looking through his glasses out across an arm of the reservoir toward a big white house that was clearly visible nearly a mile away.

Mr. Pope knew the house. It belonged to Fillson Kemmerer, president of General Utensils. But in spite of Ed's arguments he refused to see anything suspicious in what seemed to him merely idle curiosity. Ed was so insistent, however, that he finally turned off the road and rode up to where Professor Smith was standing. "Good afternoon, sir," he said. "Are you having success with your census?"

Professor Smith said yes, he was.

"I wanted to tell you," Mr. Pope said, "that just below here—tree to the left of that big pine—there is a meadowlark sitting on her nest. And if I'm not mistaken she's a rosebreasted meadowlark. But of course you'd know more about that than I would."

When Professor Smith had thanked him and hurried off down the hill, Ed said, "I find new beauties in your character every day, Wilb. I hadn't suspected you of a passionate interest in our little feathered friends. And may I ask what the hell we care about a rosy-whiskered lark or whatever it is?"

"You may," said Mr. Pope, "and I reply that the meadowlark does not nest at this time of year, nor does she nest in trees, nor is there any such bird as a rose-breasted meadowlark. Therefore—"

"Therefore the prof is a fake," said Ed. "Well, come on. What are we waiting for?"

Mr. Pope laughed. "What are you going to do—shoot him down in cold blood? We haven't anything on him. But I admit I'm curious now. Let's go back to Barney's. I want to make a couple of phone calls."

So they rode back. The first phone call confirmed their suspicions. There was no ornithologist named Smith connected with Columbia. The second call was less satisfactory. Mr. Kemmerer was away—indefinitely.

"I don't see why you called him, anyway," Ed said.

"I thought he ought to know that somebody's watching his house." He thought a minute. "I wonder what Smith's racket is. Let's ride up and look at his place."

Ed said, "You beat all, Wilb. Let a guy sabotage America and you don't do a darn thing. But let him stick a pin into a neighbor and, boy, you'll have the troops out!"

Mr. Pope grinned. "I don't think this is sabotage, Ed. The time for that has gone by. I think it's some kind of private skulduggery. Maybe we can find out what if we snoop around a little."

On the way up the dirt road they had to draw off to one side to pass a ramshackle car coming down. In the car were a man and woman who, Ed said, lived in a house at the end of the road, a short distance above Professor Smith. They could see Smith's place some time before they came to it, a small white suburban house, as innocent as a dish of mashed potatoes.

Ed made for the gate, marched through and up to the front door. Mr. Pope, with an uneasy shrug, accompanied him.

It took a good deal of urging on Ed's part to persuade Mr. Pope to dismount and peek in the window. Shading his eyes with his hand, he took a perfunctory look around a rather luxurious but quite harmless living room. "This is a darn fool business, Ed," he said. "We can't find out anything this way."

"Yeah?" said Ed, who was looking over his shoulder. "How about right under your nose there, on the desk?"

"Quit blowing down my neck," said Mr. Pope. "I don't see anything."

"That brief case, you lug. The initials on it—F. J. K. Ain't those Kemmerer's initials?"

"They are, at that." Mr. Pope became interested. "Still, it could be that—"

"Hey, come over here." Ed had moved to the window to the left, from which the other end of the desk was visible. "What do you make of those papers?"

Mr. Pope looked. "That's queer," he said. "Memo from Mr. Vail to Mr. Kemmerer. 'Production in the Buffalo plant' —hmm—lots of figures. That Buffalo plant makes tank turrets, Ed. How the devil would this fellow get hold of confidential papers—"

Crack! They had both been shoving their noses hard against the window, and all at once it gave way, and the pieces tinkled down inside the room. Ed gave a snort and backed away, then suddenly said in an urgent whisper, "Quick, Wilb! Get aboard! Company comin'!" And at the same moment Mr. Pope heard a shout from down the hill. "Hey, you! Come out of there!"

As Mr. Pope swung automatically into the saddle he saw a state trooper running up across the field below them, waving his arms. He grabbed his hat, ducked a hanging apple bough, lost a stirrup as Ed sailed over the low hedge at the back of the house, and then they were pounding on up the road.

The trooper fired twice in the air.

"That fellow means business," Ed said.

"We oughtn't to have run," complained Mr. Pope. "After all, we haven't done anything very serious."

"Listen, Wilb," Ed said. "When a cop says, 'Hey, you!' the thing to do is pick up your feet and run like hell. You follow that rule and—" He broke off as the hum of an engine grew louder behind them. "Judas, Wilb, the guy had his car with him!"

Mr. Pope would have pulled up and surrendered, but Ed kept on going. A couple of hundred yards up the hill, the road curved and ended in the barnyard of a small farmhouse, and Ed had seen that the front door of the house had been left open when its owners had driven off down the hill. The trooper was not yet in sight. Ed streaked across the barnyard and right into the open door, with Mr. Pope lying flat along his neck and protesting angrily.

"Shut the door," said Ed. "And get into them overalls. He ain't seen us close to. We can get away with it."

They were in a front hall so narrow that Mr. Pope had to dismount by sliding off over Ed's tail. There were some musty-looking work clothes hanging on pegs. Mr. Pope slid into the overalls and put on a battered hat. The car was just pulling up in the yard.

"Get out through the back," Ed said, "and be sort of puttering around. I'll stay here."

Mr. Pope found his way out through the kitchen. He picked up an axe from the block and was just starting to split some kindling when the trooper came around the side of the house.

"Where'd that guy go?" he demanded.

"What guy?" asked Mr. Pope, wiping imaginary sweat from his forehead.

"Guy on a horse just rode in here."

"On a horse, hey? Now don't it beat all what some folks'll do in the name of pleasure? You wouldn't catch me joltin' over these hills on a—"

"Did you see him or didn't you?" snapped the trooper.

"Hain't seen a soul all day, mister—barrin' you."

"Hmm." The trooper rubbed his chin. "He's got to be somewheres. I'd have seen him if he went on. Mind if I look in your barn?"

"Help yourself." Mr. Pope returned to the kindling.

Presently the trooper came back. "What's your name?" he asked.

"Jones," said Mr. Pope. "With a J," he added.

"With a J! Well, how else—"

"Some folks spell it different," said Mr. Pope. "But me, I like the old ways." He leaned on the axe and gawped with a vacant smile at his questioner.

"Ha! Smart guy!" said the trooper. "Well, I'd like to look through the house. He could have gone in there, horse and all, without you knowing it."

"Not with my wife in there, he couldn't. You don't know my wife, mister."

"No. I'd better make her acquaintance." The trooper started in the kitchen door.

Mr. Pope followed him. There was no one in the kitchen or the little parlor. The front door was closed. Mr. Pope hoped that Ed had left by it.

The trooper opened the door to a bedroom, then crossed to a door on the far side and tried it. It was locked and he shook the handle.

From behind the door came a terrible falsetto screech. "Who's there?"

"Moses!" exclaimed the trooper, then he looked sharply at Mr. Pope. "This some monkey business?"

"It's my wife," said Mr. Pope. "Hey, Minnie," he called, "there's a policeman here lookin' for a man on a horse."

"Well, he ain't in here," Ed shrieked. "I'm takin' a bath, and this tub ain't no public swimmin' pool."

The trooper stepped close to the door. "I'm sorry to disturb you, ma'am," he said, rather unsteadily, for the terrible voice had shaken him. "I was just looking around."

"And you want to look in here, hey?" Ed yelled. "Wait—I can reach out of the tub and unlock the door. Come right in, officer. Don't be bashful. It's always a pleasure to see new faces." And Ed went off into a peal of screeching laughter.

The trooper retreated into the hall, wiping his forehead. Mr. Pope followed him. "We don't see many folks up here. My wife gets kind of lonesome for company," he said apologetically.

The man eyed him dourly. "Yeah," he said. "Well, you have my sympathy, mister." He walked slowly over to his car, shaking his head.

When the trooper had gone, Mr. Pope and Ed rode back down the hill.

"I don't see how that cop happened to be there," Ed said.

"I don't think he did just happen to," said Mr. Pope. "Smith could have seen us riding up there through that spyglass of his. He could have called up the troopers."

"If he's a sabotoor he ain't askin' protection from the cops," Ed objected.

"Whatever he is, he must be pretty sure of his position," Mr. Pope said. "I think we'd better do a little telephoning."

They stopped at a tavern and Mr. Pope rang up the Kemmerer house. But Mr. Kemmerer was still away, and Mrs. Kemmerer was out and wouldn't be back for another hour. "Let's get back into our own territory," Mr. Pope said.

They were halfway across a long iron bridge that spanned an arm of the reservoir, when Ed said, "Don't look now, but here comes somebody we know."

The trooper's car had just turned onto the other end of the bridge.

"Good Lord!" said Mr. Pope. "I guess that's torn it."

"Torn it!" said Ed. "It's ripped the seat right out!"

The trooper stopped beside them. "Okay, mister," he said. "Just turn around and ride back where you came from. There's somebody up here that wants to talk to you—Mr. Jones with a J," he said sarcastically.

There was no escape this time. They clumped back off the bridge and up the side road to Professor Smith's house.

Mr. Pope dismounted. "I don't see what all this is about, officer," he protested. "It was just harmless curiosity that prompted me to look in that window. And then my foot slipped. I'll gladly have it repaired—"

"Yeah?" The trooper grinned unpleasantly. "And so you ran away. "You wouldn't have climbed in if I hadn't stopped you, I suppose?"

"Certainly not! I'm not a . . . What are you doing?" Mr. Pope demanded. For the trooper had taken a piece of string from his popcket and appeared to be measuring Ed for a pair of shoes.

"Just a little comparing," he said. He straightened up. "I suppose you've been snooping around here at night a good deal the last month? Do you deny that? There's hoof marks all over the place."

"I certainly will deny it!" But Mr. Pope knew his tone was not convincing. Ed's midnight visits had left traces which even he could see, now that he looked.

Mr. Pope went into the house, and the trooper followed. "We'll wait for the owner," he said.

They sat down in the living room. Mr. Pope noticed that the papers and briefcase had disappeared from the desk. He was pretty puzzled. If Smith was a crook, why had he called the police? "Look here," he said, "you're making a mistake. If you're going to hold anybody it ought to be this fellow Smith. In the first place that isn't his name—"

"He never told me it was. I wouldn't talk about assumed names if I were you, Mr. Jones."

The only thing to do, Mr. Pope decided, was to get in touch with the Kemmerers. Otherwise, he'd probably be jailed for housebreaking.

There was a phone on the desk. If the trooper weren't there . . . Mr. Pope got up and looked at the prints on the wall. He wandered over to the window. Ed was standing outside. Mr. Pope leaned out and called him.

"Hey!" said the trooper, jumping up. "Come back here."

"Oh, relax!" said Mr. Pope disgustedly. "I'm merely giving the horse some sugar." He felt in his pocket, then held out an empty hand to Ed, who muzzled it obligingly. He put his arm around Ed's neck and his face against Ed's cheek. Ed endured these endearments with faint disgust. Mr. Pope whispered something in his ear, gave him a pat, and went back to his chair.

Ed wandered from the window. Mr. Pope lit a cigarette and the trooper gazed stolidly at his toes. And then from somewhere outside came a series of appalling screams: "Help! Murder! Police!"

The trooper dashed out the door, and Mr. Pope snatched up the telephone receiver.

The Kemmerer butler answered his ring. Mrs. Kemmerer was still out.

"Well, give her this message immediately when she comes in. It's terribly important. Take this down—the location of this house." He gave it quickly. "Tell her to drive over here at once. No, it doesn't matter who I am. It's about Mr.

Kemmerer. I've discovered something here that—" A hand came over his shoulder and broke the connection.

Mr. Pope sat back and looked up into the face of Professor Smith. But when he spoke, his voice had a brisk authority that the professor's had lacked at their previous meetings. "Well, you detectives are smarter than I gave you credit for being. And yet not so smart either. You might have made a much more profitable deal with me. But of course, now that you have called my wife—"

"I'm not a detective," said Mr. Pope. Then he frowned. "What do you mean, I called your wife?"

"You mean you don't know who I am?" Professor Smith demanded incredulously. "You mean you're just a common snooper who's stumbled on . . . Oh, good God!" Then, with a nasty smile: "Well, I have some influence. I shall certainly see that Westchester is deprived permanently of one of its more inquisitive residents."

"You'll do as you see fit about that," said Mr. Pope with dignity. "I've done what I thought right. When a man calling himself John Smith pretends—" He broke off as the trooper reentered the room.

"Oh, you're back, sir," said the man. "Somebody yelling bloody murder out there a minute ago, but there's no one there now. Kids, I suppose."

"Never mind that," said Professor Smith. "This man has just phoned my wife. She'll probably be here in a little while. You might as well get along, Otis. We'll drop the house-breaking charge. There are better ways of dealing with this fellow."

As the trooper went out a light illuminated the muddled darkness of Mr. Pope's brain. "You're Fillson Kemmerer!" he exclaimed.

"Of course I am, you damned fool," the other snapped. "But you've done yourself no service by finding it out. If it's through you I have to go back to that cursed atmosphere of dim lights and ectoplasm and—"

Mr. Pope interrupted firmly. "Wait a minute. Yes, I see you're Mr. Kemmerer now. The beard and the limp threw me off. If I've made a mistake I'm willing to rectify it. And I think I can, too. But I've got to know more than I do. You're living here as Smith. I assume it is your daughter who brings you things at night and keeps you in touch. You're probably also in touch with your business. But not with your wife. Why?"

Kemmerer glared angrily, then he shrugged and dropped into a chair. "Very well. It can do no harm now. And if you can rectify your mistake . . . not that I believe it for a minute. No matter what story you tell my wife when she comes, she'll be suspicious. She's already hired detectives to find me, and they'll be swarming all over the place. Up to now they've been looking for me in California, I imagine, since I talked a good deal about California before I left."

"We're wasting time," Mr. Pope put in quietly.

"Very well. My wife, Mr. ah—?"

"Pope."

"—Mr. Pope, has in the past few years gone in very heavily for spiritualism. Her friends are no longer my friends; they are mediaeval monks, Babylonian princesses, and the ghosts of half-witted children. My home life is lived in a dim world of whispers and sudden cold draughts, of clammy fingers on the back of the neck and *Abide With Me* sung off-key in darkened rooms. When I come back from the city there are stout vulgar women in the library and turbaned dark-skinned gentlemen having tea on the terrace."

"I see. There are swamis at the bottom of the garden," Mr. Pope murmured. "And so, sir, you left home?"

"I had no choice. My friends would no longer come to the house. Why, the place was so overrun with these people that even in your bed you weren't free from them. I am as interested as the next man in historical personages, but a voice from under the bed which announces itself as the spirit of Queen Victoria wishing your opinion of Palmerston's foreign policy at two a. m.—well, I ask you!"

"They were very anxious to convert you," Mr. Pope said.

"And they came very near it. I often wondered if, instead of dropping off to sleep, I wasn't slipping into a trance myself. And so, with the connivance of my daughter and a few friends, I quietly disappeared." He looked hard at Mr. Pope. "You are wondering why I didn't simply put my foot down and throw these people out of my house. I can only say, you don't know my wife."

"There's been nothing in the papers," said Mr. Pope. "I take it she doesn't want publicity, and so hasn't gone to the police." Kemmerer nodded. "Well . . ." Mr. Pope got up and looked out the window. Ed, leaning nonchalantly against a tree, raised inquiring eyebrows. The hum of a car came up the hill. Mr. Pope swung round. "That'll be your wife now.

You'd better clear out, sir. Keep well away from the house. Please! The least you can do is to give me a chance!"

"Very well." Kemmerer allowed himself to be hustled through the back door. "But if you fail . . ."

Mr. Pope had had no plan. He had been playing for time, and now that all the time was gone and action was called for, he felt pretty discouraged. To deny that he had phoned her was useless. Her attention was now focused on this house; she wouldn't be put off with some cock-and-bull story of his having seen her husband in Omaha or San Diego. The only hope was the spiritualist angle, yet he doubted if any performance he could put on would deceive even a child.

He heard the car stop in the yard. He groaned and went out. A chauffeur opened the car door and a tall woman stepped out. "I am Mrs. Kemmerer," she said. "You are the man who phoned?"

Looking at her, Mr. Pope understood very well why her husband had not put his foot down. He could never have taken it up again quickly enough to avoid having his toes crushed. Under iron-gray hair her blunt face had a sort of unfinished look, as if the material had been too tough and the artist had given up in despair. He would have to put on an awfully good show.

He bowed. "Yes, madam. Will you please come in?"

She hesitated a moment, then preceded him into the living room. As he pulled forward a chair for her, she turned and said, "Where is my husband?"

"My dear Mrs. Kemmerer," Mr. Pope protested. "I have no precise information, I am afraid. My voices have, however, indicated in a general way his present whereabouts. It was only this afternoon that I received the communication. I hastened to inform you—"

"Just what are you talking about? I understood you were one of O'Donnell's men? You didn't leave your name, but you telephoned that you had information—"

"I am not a detective," said Mr. Pope. "I am a medium. An amateur, it is true, but the voices from beyond the veil do not speak solely to those who exhibit them for money. I seek no reward—"

"Balderdash!" she snapped. "Your voices may or may not give authentic information on spiritual matters, but when I want to know what is going on in *this* world I employ detectives."

"You astound me, madam," Mr. Pope said. "You are known as an earnest seeker for the truths that lie beneath appearances. Yet when an authentic message is offered you—"

"You seem to be under the impression, young man," she cut in, "that I am a credulous old woman. Let me assure you that I am quite aware that ninety per cent of you people are charlatans. If it amuses me to search among you for the occasional grains of truth—" She broke off. "How did you learn that my husband had disappeared?" she demanded.

"My voices—the voices that speak to me in the silent watches of the night."

"Fiddlesticks!" She glowered at him. "You are very stupid to try to bamboozle me with that cheap high-flown talk. That alone assures me that no message of yours would be of the slightest interest to me." She turned to leave.

And a great roaring voice suddenly boomed, "No interest, hey? Beware, rash mortal! Where were you at ten o'clock on the night of July 15th, 1923?"

"Wh-what's that?" Mrs. Kemmerer swung around, just as Ed's head disappeared from the window.

"Did you hear it too?" said Mr. Pope. "Usually I am the only one that hears it." She eyed him with grim suspicion. "What do you know about the night of July whatever-it-is?"

What does Ed know, is the point, Mr. Pope thought. For it had visibly shaken her. He said, "I am only the medium, madam. You will know better than I what the voice refers to."

"We'll have a look at your voice," she snapped, and going to the door, called her chauffeur, whom she instructed to search the house, inside and out, for a loud speaker and a confederate. Mr. Pope said nothing. He lit a cigarette, walked to the window and gave Ed, who was still standing outside, an approving wink.

The chauffeur had evidently had previous experience in unmasking impostors. Every piece of furniture, every inch of floor and wall space in the living room, and then in every other room, was examined. Then he went outside.

"I should not have sent for you, madam," Mr. Pope said, "if I had expected to find you so skeptical. You have angered the Captain, and he is likely to make disclosures concerning you which you would prefer not to have revealed. But that is his way—"

"What captain?" she demanded.

"He is the spirit of an old pirate captain who was hanged

at Execution Dock in 1753. I have always found his messages reliable. That is why, when he mentioned seeing your husband, I phoned you."

The chauffeur came back to report that he had found nothing. "There is no one on the premises but ourselves, madam, and no wires or amplifying device of any kind."

"Very well, Bates. It is evidently some trick with which we are not familiar. If—"

"Trick, hey?" roared the voice. "Why you lead-keeled, barnacle-bottomed old windjammer, I'll show you tricks! I'll—"

"Come, come, Captain," put in Mr. Pope. "Take it easy."

The chauffeur, his face the color of lard, backed slowly out through the door. Mrs. Kemmerer dropped into a chair. "Very well," she said. "I accept your explanation. But only provisionally. It is true, I have sometimes seen things that I would not have believed possible. Perhaps this is one of them."

"Perhaps," he said, "you wouldn't like to ask the Captain some questions?"

"She don't need to ask no questions," bawled Ed. "She wants to know where her husband is, ain't that it? Mostly that's what they want to know. Well, the last time I see the durn little squirt, he was settin' under an umbrella on some white sand. Now wait a minute, ma'am, till I take a squint at my crystal ball. Yeah, there he sets, with nothin' on but a pair of little pants, and a glass with somethin' pink in it in one hand, and—tut, tut, what's this? Wimmin—my lord! Why, they ought to be ashamed of theirselves, the hussies! Man and boy, I've sailed the seven seas for forty year, but I never seen nothin' to equal this here display of—"

Mr. Pope said hastily, "Never mind the description, Captain. Let's have a better location than just a strip of beach."

"'Strip' is the word," Ed roared jovially. "Well, lemme see —latitude 34 north, longitude 118 west, as near as I can figure."

"That should be California," said Mr. Pope. "Southern Los Angeles, I'd guess, or thereabouts."

Mrs. Kemmerer shook her head irritably. "I don't understand this, Mr.—ah—this vulgar burlesque of— And yet—whatever the value of your information, you have produced a phenomenon for which I have no explanation. Well, is that all he can tell me?"

"No, it ain't," roared the Captain. "I can tell you about that night of July—"

"That's enough!" She got up quickly. "Thank you. I—" She turned and hurried toward the door. "Thank you."

"Them hard-boiled ones are always the biggest suckers," Ed said, when the car had driven off down the hill.

"I guess that's so," Mr. Pope said. "But if it hadn't been for that stuff about ten o'clock on July 15th—that's what shook her. Where'd you get that, Ed?"

"Shot in the dark." Ed giggled. "Forty years ago—she wouldn't remember exact dates, you know—but she'd have been in her twenties then. And you can bet there was some evenin's those days she wouldn't want folks to know what she was up to. Why, you just think back yourself, Wilb."

"Yeah," said Mr. Pope. "I guess you're right. I guess she won't ever come back here again. She'll just think I'm a charlatan who knew she was interested in spiritualism, and was trying to cash in. But what do we tell Kemmerer?"

What he told Kemmerer a few minutes later was not very convincing. He had persuaded her, by means of a fake séance. . . .

"Nonsense," said Mr. Kemmerer. "My wife is not gullible, Mr. Pope. She has exposed more mediums than Houdini ever did. If you think—"

"Avast there, you cat-whiskered rosy-breasted swab!" came Ed's roaring voice. "Where were you at ten o'clock on the night of July 15th, 1923? Hey? Answer me that!"

Kemmerer dashed to the window, looked out, then swung round. "How the devil did you do that?"

"Just a trick," said Mr. Pope modestly. "That's what worked on your wife. You see—"

"No, no," interrupted Kemmerer. "I don't care how you did it. What was that date again? You actually asked her—"

"Why, yes. About July 15th, 1923."

"The fifteenth? Yes, it could be. . . ." Kemmerer's mouth fell open. "Oh, my lord! . . . See here, I want to know—"

"Want to know what? Want me to tell you where you were that night?" The big voice roared with laughter which seemed to shake the room, and Mr. Kemmerer flinched.

"Er—no," he said hastily, and with a suspicious look at Mr. Pope. "I'm simply wondering if I can rely on your discretion?"

"Good Lord," said Mr. Pope, "I'm not trying to butt into

something's none of my business. Only to make sure that Mrs. Kemmerer doesn't return here."

Mr. Kemmerer said impatiently, "Yes, yes. Let's not beat about the bush. You have indeed done me a great service." He had recovered his good humor, and now he smiled a little one-sidedly. "You could have struck nothing more effective. Yes, you win the stuffed rosy-breasted meadowlark, nest and all!" He smiled more widely. "Oh yes, I was not fooled by that, I should tell you. You see, I really am interested in migrants. But you do pull the right numbers out of the hat sometimes, you do, indeed! Nineteen-twenty-three! My word!"

"What in thunder, Ed," said Mr. Pope as they rode homeward, "do you suppose happened on that date of yours?"

"I guess you never suspected, Wilb," said Ed, "that I had them natural psychic powers, did you? We might have a little séance when we get home, and I'll take another peek into my crystal ball."

"Let's have our séance at Barney's and peek into a glass of beer," said Mr. Pope. "That's where your inspiration comes from, mostly."

"Ain't that the truth!" said Ed.

Ed Gets a Mother Complex

If you didn't know the inside facts like I do most all you could say about that horse of Mr. Pope's was that he was a horse. People in Mt. Kisco used to laugh like anything when he went clumping by with Mr. Pope sort of crouched on his back and some of them even got mad about it. My goodness they said that Wilbur Pope must make forty thousand a year and he's got a fine house and a wife that makes most other women look as if they'd just been rescued from drowning and he ought to be ashamed to ride around on that revolting old plug! But Mr. Pope didn't care. He'd bought this horse so that weekends he could get out where it was quiet instead of staying home and pouring drinks for Mrs. Pope's friends. And he got pretty fond of him. The horse's name was Ed.

Well of course plenty of men have horses or dogs they are fond of and even prefer to human society and it's easy to see why. A horse will never give you an argument, and a dog will listen to your troubles without interrupting to squawk about his own sufferings. He's man's best friend because he has no comeback. But Ed could talk. And in spite of that Mr. Pope was fond of him. Ed had his opinions and they were good sensible ones though perhaps sometimes his language was a little coarse. But Mr. Pope had been to college so he didn't mind that.

Of course Ed's being able to talk was sometimes embarrassing. Like the time Mr. Pope went to that auction up near Mt. Kisco. They'd been out riding that Saturday and had stopped in several taverns for beer. They'd had enough for the time being and were sort of ambling up a back road when they came to a white house on a hill and a lot of cars around it and about forty people sitting on the lawn in undertakers' chairs in front of a man who was standing on a table and yelling. Everything in the house had been brought out and stacked on the porch and I don't suppose it was any funnier a lot of junk than your or my personal

66

"This is your horse?"

property would be if it was all dragged out into the sunshine but Ed and Mr. Pope thought it was funny and they went and stood under a tree a little back from the crowd and watched.

Well the first thing they saw sold was a glass dish which the auctioneer said was a hobnail pattern and a genuine antique and the bidding started at a quarter and went right up to ten dollars and ten cents. Jeez it must be an antique at that said Ed though what anybody'd want with a dish with warts all over it I dunno. The woman who'd bought it turned around and looked angrily at Mr. Pope and Ed laughed and said something which I can't repeat because it was slightly off color and the woman didn't turn around again but sat up very straight and her ears got red. Shut up you fool! whispered Mr. Pope. Everybody thinks I said that and I'm not going to have your smart cracks fathered on me. Smut cracks Wilb—smut cracks said Ed and began to giggle. Not bad, hey? he said. Just one more good or bad and we go home said Mr. Pope crossly so Ed didn't say any more.

Well the next thing put up was a steeple clock which was all right but you couldn't wind it up but it was a genuine antique too and went for fifteen and then came a genuine antique chair with no seat in it that went for twelve dollars. What's all this antique stuff Wilb? said Ed in a low voice. If these folks want stuff that's busted and won't work why don't they stay home and bust their own clocks and kick the seats out of their own chairs and save their money? Collectors said Mr. Pope. They'll collect anything. Joe Fisher in my office has got a collection of two hundred baby carriages. And for collectors' purposes anything that isn't made any more is an antique. Yeah? said Ed. Well they quit making silk stockings a while back. Let's you and me start a collection of them. Some fun, hey? O look he said what's the guy got now?

The next thing was a parlor organ in good condition except that it wheezed badly when the auctioneer played a few chords on it. The bidding started at a dollar and went rapidly up to five dollars and a half and it was sort of hesitating there when Ed yelled suddenly Five seventy-five!

Five seventy-five from the gentleman with the horse said the auctioneer and he's a musician himself or I miss my guess for he's got a voice could sing *Asleep in the Deep* to the queen's taste. Everybody laughed because Ed had yelled his bid in a voice that could have been heard over on the other side of the hill. For heaven's sake Ed! murmured Mr. Pope. Do I hear six? said the auctioneer. Six I have. Do I hear the quarter? Six and a quarter I have. Do I hear the half? You sir? He looked at Mr. Pope who shook his head.

The organ sold finally for nine dollars and when attention had turned to a tin foot bath filled with old books Mr. Pope said What on earth got into you Ed? I dunno said Ed. I thought it would be kind of nice to have in the stable and you could accompany me and I could sing some of the old songs. It would go with your voice all right said Mr. Pope with that wheeze in it. And how did you suppose we'd get it home? Hadn't thought of that said Ed. Well said Mr. Pope you'd better think of it.

So Ed was quiet for a while but Mr. Pope could see that he was getting auction fever which comes upon even hardboiled old plugs like Ed and makes them lose all sense of values and bid as long as anybody can be found to bid against them. Come on Ed let's be going said Mr. Pope but Ed was too intent on the bidding to hear him. And suddenly he shouted Twenty-five!

Well it was a picture Ed was bidding on and it was pretty terrible. It showed a square-headed little girl with curls sitting in a big chair with spectacles on and a smirk and the name of it was *I'se Dram'ma*. Ed for heaven's sake! said Mr. Pope. Cute ain't it? said Ed and as an old gentleman with tobacco-stained whiskers raised the bid to three with a truculent look at Mr. Pope the horse called Three-fifty!

But when the old gentleman went to four Mr. Pope shook his head violently at the auctioneer. Going at four dollars— last call said the auctioneer but Mr. Pope was staring menacingly at Ed who didn't dare bid again. Aw what's the matter with you Wilbur? said Ed as the next picture *A Yard of Pansies* was put up. My gosh four dollars! It isn't the four dollars and you know it said Mr. Pope but I'm not going to ride home like a border reiver with the spoils of war in the shape of *I'se Dram'ma* at my saddle bow. You might better come home with some nice pictures said Ed than with some other things. I guess your wife would rather see you roll home with *I'se Dram'ma* than with a load of Old Grandad like you did last Sunday. That was a right pretty picture but if you grudge four dollars for me to have something like that hung up over my stall to give me pleasure I got nothing more to say. Fine said Mr. Pope if you've got nothing more to say we'll stay.

Well there were several more pictures that went up after that but though Ed wanted to bid on *Cupid Awake and Cupid Asleep* and on a steel engraving of *The Wreck of the Hesperus* Mr. Pope wouldn't let him.

At this point there was some innocent gaiety caused by the tobacco-stained old gentleman who bought what he thought was a bundle of pillow cases which when opened turned out to be six pairs of old-fashioned drawers trimmed with Hamburg lace. Hell I can't never take them things home! he said and began distributing them to the ladies in his vicinity most of whom took the joke in good part. But one large pink woman in a garden hat stared coldly at the ribald old gentleman and said I do not think that is funny. You and her Wilb muttered Ed. My gosh what do folks come to an auction for if it isn't to have some fun? Don't pout said Mr. Pope it isn't becoming. Anyway he said I don't want to spoil your fun. But I know that woman. It won't do to have her telling everybody that I'm eccentric and a lot of things would look eccentric to her that you and I would think were fun. Like buying *I'se Dram'ma*. She hasn't much humor in her. Yeah said Ed I know what you're trying to say. You're ashamed of me. You want to get out of here because you're ashamed of being seen by her with an old nag like me.

Mr. Pope turned and looked at the horse. Say what's the matter with you Ed? he said. He hesitated a minute and then took hold of the bridle and led Ed over close to where Mrs. Lamson was sitting. How do you do Mrs. Lamson? he said. Mrs. Lamson turned and smiled graciously. O how do you do Mr. Pope? she said. I thought I saw you over there. You've been riding? Mr. Pope said yes he rode a good deal weekends. How nice said Mrs. Lamson and then she looked at Ed and frowned slightly. And this is—er—your horse? Mr. Pope said it was. He wished Ed would stand up straighter and not leer. He was sure that Ed was standing knockkneed on purpose.

I used to hunt a great deal said Mrs. Lamson. I was practically brought up on horseback. Back home in the Genesee Valley. She had plainly dismissed Ed from consciousness. She was talking about horses now—not about Ed. Therefore Ed is not a horse—Q.E.D. said Mr. Pope to himself. I never rode much he said until I bought Ed. But I enjoy it very much. There's a great deal of pleasure in having a good horse. O a good horse—yes said Mrs. Lamson. Then she said I gather you're interested in antiques?

Mr. Pope wasn't sure whether she had changed the subject or not but he said O no he had just been passing by and stopped out of curiosity. Mrs. Lamson said There is nothing of any value here—except possibly that breakfront. But the rest of this rubbish! She made what in her girlhood she had practiced as a little *moue*. Nowadays it was just a face. Mr. Pope led Ed back to the shade of his tree.

I take it all back said Ed. You wasn't ashamed of me. Just the same you ought to slapped her down the cracks she made. What the hell is a breakfront Wilb? Search me said Mr. Pope. But see here Ed. If you want to buy something so much I won't stop you. Provided it's something we can carry home. You mean that? said Ed. And when Mr. Pope said Yes he said Boy then you're going to see some action.

Well the first thing Ed bid on was a feather bed which he thought would be more comfortable to sleep on than the rather inferior grade of straw which he accused Mr. Pope of providing for him. Or I could wear it over my shoulders winter mornings he said—like a sort of negligee. But the ribald old gentleman bid on it too and Ed had taken a fancy to him after the episode of the drawers so he let him have it.

And then the auctioneer put up a picture of a race horse. This is a hand-painted oil painting ladies and gentlemen he said and I don't know when I've seen a nicer painted one. Almost clear and sharp as a colored photograph. Who'll say a dollar to start it? A dollar! called Ed.

Why didn't you say a quarter you dope murmured Mr. Pope. No sense throwing my money away. I'd be ashamed to make such a bid said Ed. Well I don't see—Mr. Pope began. It reminds me of my mother said Ed simply. O said Mr. Pope I beg your pardon Ed.

Somebody bid two dollars and Ed promptly bid three. Three from the gentleman over by the tree said the auctioneer and if I may say so sir the horse in this picture kind of favors that horse of yours—she does indeed. Everyone turned around and there was some laughter. I expect maybe when you were young said Mr. Pope looking thoughtfully at Ed. What was your mother's name? And when Ed said it was

Nellie he called to the auctioneer and asked him if there was any name on the picture. Something here on the back said the man. Here 'tis—Jenny Lind—owned by Colonel E. P. Rockway. Four dollars. Four and a half. Do I hear the five?

Not your mother after all said Mr. Pope. Yeah? said Ed. Well I guess I ought to know my own mother. Far as I know she never stood for her portrait. Too busy on the milk route. But folks always said she was pretty as a picture and this must be the picture she was as pretty as. Had four white stockings just like the picture too. Well you were going to collect stockings said Mr. Pope so here's your chance. But I guess somebody else has got the same idea. For the bids had now reached six dollars. Half! called Ed. Well someone bid seven and Ed went the half and they bid eight and Ed went the half again and Mr. Pope said Gosh Ed! and then he shrugged his shoulders and said O well I can take it. And then all at once he saw that the person who was bidding against Ed was Mrs. Lamson.

Well Mr. Pope did not realize for a minute that Mrs. Lamson had turned around and was beckoning to him. So just as Ed had gotten up to twelve dollars he walked over to her. I just realized she said that it is you who are bidding against me. Have you a particular reason for wanting to own this picture Mr. Pope? Why it's on account of Ed said Mr. Pope and then as she looked puzzled he said That is Ed is my horse you know and as the picture looked rather like him— I can't see that it looks particularly like him interrupted Mrs. Lamson and so as it seems to be merely a whim of yours to bid it up I will tell you that I want to bid it in for my collection. You see when harness racing was so popular most of the old time trotters had their portraits painted and I've been able to find a great many of them.

I have twelve madam said the auctioneer catching her eye. Will you bid thirteen? Just a moment said Mrs. Lamson and turned back to Mr. Pope. I found a portrait of Maud S last week she said. She held the record in 1885—two minutes eight and three quarters seconds. I'm extremely anxious to get Jenny Lind. She held the record only part of one season and so not being a famous horse like Goldsmith Maid for instance it seemed unlikely that there would be a portrait. Well in that case said Mr. Pope. Thank you said Mrs. Lamson I felt sure you'd be reasonable about it. Thirteen! she called.

But as Mr. Pope walked back to where he had left Ed standing under a tree the horse bid fifteen.

Mrs. Lamson turned in angry amazement. Sixteen! she said. Stop it you fool! muttered Mr. Pope. Twenty! shouted Ed. Twenty-one! said Mrs. Lamson. Twenty-five and I've only begun to bid! yelled Ed.

Mrs. Lamson got up and turned around and walked slowly over to Mr. Pope. You can have it Mr. Pope she said furiously. But I think you will regret it. And she walked off to her car.

Mr. Pope didn't say anything to Ed until they were a mile or two along the road home. He had looped his arm through the wire on the back of the picture which he was carrying like a shield. Well he said finally you fixed me all right. O shucks Wilb don't be such a sourpuss said Ed. What's twenty-five bucks to a man in your position? I haven't got any position said Mr. Pope—not after she tells Lamson that I said I'd let her have the picture and then went on bidding. Hell you saved him twenty dollars said Ed. He's an advertising man said Mr. Pope. He believes you should encourage people to spend—not save. Why couldn't you have kept your mouth shut? I dunno said the horse. I guess it was when she said you were just bidding it in for a whim and you let her get away with it. It ain't any whim wanting my own mother's picture. Sounds like a whim to me said Mr. Pope. All right said Ed all right—call it a whim then. But if it had been me in your place and your mother's picture I'd promised to buy for you believe me I'd have bought it. If I make a promise I keep it whim or no whim. My whim is as good as my bond. Well what you kicking about? said Mr. Pope. The picture's yours.

So they got the picture home and into the stable without Mrs. Pope seeing it and hung it over Ed's manger. And that evening Mrs. Pope looked out the window and said Wilbur you left the light on in the stable. So I did said Mr. Pope because he didn't want to tell her that Ed had probably turned the light on so he could see his new family portrait. Well go turn it out said Mrs. Pope. O let it burn said Mr. Pope. What's two cents' worth of electricity? But Mrs. Pope gave a sniff and before he could stop her went out to the stable. And in a minute she called Wilbur Wilbur!

So Mr. Pope went after her. What's this picture over Ed's manger? said Mrs. Pope. O said Mr. Pope I bought that for Ed. I thought it would sort of—you know—dress up the place for him. Dress it up for him! exclaimed Mrs. Pope. A horse! Wilbur have you gone stark staring— But

she didn't get any further because just then Carrie came out
to tell them that they had callers.

Well Mr. Pope was glad for the interruption but he wasn't
so glad when they went into the house and found Mr. and
Mrs. Lamson there. Good evening Mr. Pope said Mrs. Lamson. We've come over to see if we can't come to some agree-
ment about that picture. I've talked it over with Mr. Lamson
and we both feel that we want to be fair and that perhaps you
didn't understand— What is all this Wilbur? said Mrs. Pope.
So Mrs. Lamson explained. Well goodness Wilbur said
Mrs. Pope if you told Mrs. Lamson you weren't going to bid
against her and then went right ahead with your bidding the
only decent thing to do is give the picture to her. Mr.
Lamson didn't say anything but just looked as he did when
there was trouble in the office.

Well Mr. Pope was in a quandary not to say a dilemma
but he saw all at once that there was one thing he could not
do—he could not let Ed down. For Ed was his friend but
Mr. Lamson was just a rich neighbor. So he said I'm sorry but
I'm afraid I can't give the picture to you Mrs. Lamson because it doesn't belong to me now. I bought it to give to a
friend and I've already given it to him. Why Wilbur— Mrs.
Pope began but Mr. Pope said Please Carlotta! and so she
didn't say any more but she made up her mind she'd say
plenty as soon as the Lamsons were gone.

So then Mr. Lamson spoke for the first time. Perhaps if
your friend knows the circumstances he said—if he knows
how important it is for Mrs. Lamson and—he added after a
slight pause—for you to have the matter settled in a friendly
way—perhaps he'd be willing to give it up. Mr. Pope said
doubtfully that he might and then he said if they'd wait a few
minutes he'd go ask him. And he went down to the stable.

But Ed had no intention of giving the picture up. Go
ahead he said angrily Go ahead! Give the old fool the picture.
Don't let *my* feelings stand in your way. Don't bother about
me. I'm only a horse. I'm only the one you gave the picture
to. If you want to be an Indian giver I can't stop you. O gosh
Ed said Mr. Pope be reasonable will you? I'll get you another horse picture—I'll get you half a dozen. I don't want
any others said Ed. Would you trade your own mother's
picture in for that of some other old plug? Don't be rude
said Mr. Pope and anyway she isn't your mother. Jenny Lind
ran in the seventies and your mother couldn't have been

alive then. Well so it's my grandmother then said Ed. What's the difference? *I'se Dram'ma* murmured Mr. Pope. But Ed looked up at the picture and said in a husky voice I never knew my mother Wilb. I missed all that—the tender care a mother lavishes on her little son. And this—this lifeless picture—it cannot speak to me—tell me all the loving things that she must have murmured to me when I was too young to understand. Yet it is all I have of her Wilbur. Would you take even that away from me?

O gosh Ed said Mr. Pope exasperatedly you know perfectly well she's not your mother. I can't be mistaken said Ed shaking his head. Instinctively one recognizes his own. Rats! said Mr. Pope. Rats for you no doubt said Ed. Horses for me. No no Wilbur he went on this surge of filial emotion I feel when I gaze upon that picture—

He rolled his eyes sentimentally then choked up and a large tear slid down his long nose. And just as Mr. Pope started to reply Mr. Lamson's voice behind him said Ah there you are Wilbur. We had to be getting along and Mrs. Pope said she thought we'd find you here. Has your horse got a cold? he asked as Ed gave a loud sniff. I'm sorry to be so long Mr. Pope began but Mrs. Lamson rushed forward. Why there's Jenny Lind! she exclaimed. O then you have her back! No said Mr. Pope unfortunately I haven't. My friend refuses to give it up. May we ask your friend's name? said Mr. Lamson but Mr. Pope said No he'd prefer not because it wouldn't be any use.

See here Wilbur said Mr. Lamson you must realize that this all has a rather unpleasant look to us. You say the picture has been given away yet we find it in your possession. You refuse to give the name of the owner. You don't explain why you continued to bid after promising that you wouldn't. I don't like that Wilbur. Nevertheless I am prepared to overlook all this and to offer you exactly twice what you paid for the picture—fifty dollars. Is it a deal? Mr. Pope looked Mr. Lamson straight in the eye and said No!

Well Mr. Lamson looked at Mrs. Lamson and they both began to swell up as if they were going to explode but before they could Carrie came out and said Mr. Pope was wanted on the phone. So he went in and it was a Mr. Sproul who said he'd learned that Mr. Pope had bought a picture of Jenny Lind. Mr. Pope said Yes he had and Mr. Spoul said Well I intended to go to the auction and bid on that picture but I was detained but I think I can make you an attractive offer for it. And when Mr. Pope said it wasn't for sale Mr. Sproul said Well he could go to $250.

Well when Mr. Pope heard that he swallowed and said it did indeed sound attractive and he might consider it only would Mr. Sproul mind telling him just why he wanted it. Mr. Sproul said not at all for he was a dealer and he had several clients who were collecting portraits of early trotters and while some horse portraits were fairly common this was the only known portrait of Jenny Lind. So Mr. Pope said he'd call him in the morning and went back to the barn.

Well Wilbur said Mr. Lamson is this answer of yours final? Mr. Pope glanced at Ed who was looking kind of worried and the horse shook his head at him but Mr. Pope said Absolutely final. Very good said Mr. Lamson, but I believe this terminates our friendship. Well that's all right with me for I don't particularly care to be friends with a man who would try to pull a fast one on his neighbor. I don't understand you said Mr. Lamson. Perhaps it will clear it up for you if you tell me why Mrs. Lamson didn't raise my last bid said Mr. Pope. Why what perfect nonsense! said Mrs. Lamson. Is it? said Mr. Pope turning to her. I suggest he said that you thought I did not know the real value of this picture and that you stopped bidding because you thought Mr. Lamson could buy it from me at a fraction of its worth. Why I never heard anything so ridiculous! said Mrs. Lamson. What do you think it is worth? Well said Mr. Pope I would consider an offer of three hundred dollars. Well everybody gasped including Ed but Mr. Lamson who had been looking more and more worried put his arm on Mr. Pope's shoulder and gave a laugh that would have been jovial if it hadn't cracked badly in the middle and said By George Wilbur you caught us out nicely and I must say you have passed our little test with flying colors. What little test? said Mr. Pope and Mr. Lamson said so I arranged this little test with Mrs. Lamson. I made it obvious that we were trying to force a bad bargain on you but you saw through it and then turned the tables neatly. I congratulate you my boy. And we are offering three hundred dollars for that picture.

Mr. Pope thought a minute and then he said H'm yes—I see. But my business sense still tells me that it would be a mistake to close tonight. Suppose I give you my answer tomorrow? So Mr. Lamson said that would be fine and Mrs.

Lamson looked sort of bewildered but she said good night politely when Mr. Lamson nudged her and they went.

Why Wilbur! said Mrs. Pope I thought you were— Why you were wonderful! I was indeed said Mr. Pope. But right now I need a drink so let's go in. Ed coughed meaningly but Mr. Pope went on out of the barn. But a little later he came back with a bottle and gave Ed a generous slug of whiskey. Boy that's the stuff! said Ed. Got a wallop to it like having a tree fall on you. Where'd you get it? It's Old Stormy said Mr. Pope. Fifteen years old and I can get it for three-fifty a bottle. If I hadn't spent so much for that picture of your mother today I could get us a few bottles tomorrow. Yeah said Ed but the picture's mine now. All yours agreed Mr. Pope. But of course if you took Lamson's offer—let's see—after paying me back you'd have two hundred and seventy-five dollars. That would be—hell I'm no business man—around eighty bottles. Eighty bottles said Ed dreamily. You know Wilb he said I've been thinking—this talk about a mother's influence and as the twig is bent and so on—well it's all a lot of baloney. I ain't saying anything against mothers. They're all right in their place and I suppose you have to have 'em. But this is a man's world. So I've heard said Mr. Pope. Yeah said Ed and too much mother's influence turns out sissies. All this crying into your beer because you never had a mother's care . . . Well look at me—I turned out all right without it didn't I? I guess you wouldn't have been any different said Mr. Pope.

Ed looked at him suspiciously for a minute then turned and looked up at the portrait. I dunno Wilb he said. Something seems to have gone out of that picture for me. Now if it was really my mother's picture— Instinctively one recognizes one's own murmured Mr. Pope. Well a guy can be mistaken can't he? said Ed. O K said Mr. Pope let's take it down and I'll accept Lamson's offer for you. Maybe it would be better said Ed. Keep it here and it would only soften me up all the time. And we can't afford to be soft life being what it is. When can you get delivery on that liquor Wilb?

Ed Takes the Cockeyed Initiative

When Mrs. Pope's Aunt Amelia died Mr. Pope didn't feel very bad. How could he?—he'd never even seen her. Of course I don't mean that he felt good about it either. All of Aunt Amelia's money went to her stepson Laurence Hammersley. And although she had left instructions that her famous string of pearls should go to Mrs. Pope there wasn't much for Mr. Pope to feel gay about in that because while they would look nice on Mrs. Pope he knew she would look just as nice in a ten-cent store string which didn't have to be insured for $10,000. So as I say he didn't feel either one way or the other about it and he wore a black necktie and looked solemn for a day or two and that was that.

Of course Mrs. Pope went to the funeral which was in Philadelphia and when she got back to Mt. Kisco Mr. Pope asked her about the pearls. O I expect Laurence will send them along soon said Mrs. Pope. But didn't you ask him about them? said Mr. Pope and Mrs. Pope said Why Wilbur at a time like that you can't talk about such things. And Mr. Pope said O.

Well a month went by and nothing was heard from Mr. Hammersley. Mrs. Pope wondered about the pearls some but Mr. Pope didn't say anything because the longer she didn't have them the longer he wouldn't have to pay insurance on them. But finally a letter came and in it Mr. Hammersley said that in a couple of weeks he was coming up to New York and he would like to see the Popes. So Mrs. Pope wrote and invited him to spend a week in Mt. Kisco.

Well I guess Mrs. Pope would have been more irritated about not getting the pearls if she hadn't had something else to be irritated about. This something else was a man who had taken the Haight place. His name was Jelks. But Mrs. Pope didn't mind this so much. What she minded was that the Haight place—which was a three-room stone cottage with a big studio—was shoved right tight up against the

Ed usually seemed to be standing close to the hedge.

Pope place so that if you sat in the Haight garden when the Popes were in their garden you were practically a member of the Pope family circle. And Mr. Jelks was not possessed of those endearing qualities which might make him acceptable as a member. He was a wiry young-old man with a derisive expression which was at once reinforced and made ambiguous by a bad squint. And it was his pleasure to sit in his garden in the cool of the evening and stare at the Popes—now and then laughing quietly to himself.

Mr. Pope maintained that Mr. Jelks was merely smiling gently at his own thoughts. Mrs. Pope said she didn't doubt it and that merely showed what kind of man he was to have that kind of thoughts. And as for staring at you said Mr. Pope nobody but a trained oculist could tell what he was staring at. You could tell quickly enough if you wanted to said Mrs. Pope. Maybe you don't mind that gargoyle sitting there snickering at us but if you had any consideration for me you'd make him stop it. O come Carlotta said Mr. Pope you can't prevent him sitting in his own garden. I admit he's a nuisance but I understand he's only taken the place for two months. We can put up with him that long. Mrs. Pope said she guessed she'd have if her husband was too big a coward to protect her from insults. But Mr. Pope didn't see what he could do.

Ed had no use for Mr. Jelks either and he had even less for his man Tom. Tom was a big jovial red-faced man and although he cooked and made beds and answered the door, he called Mr. Jelks Pete which isn't standard practice between servant and employer in Mt. Kisco. Ed objected to that and he objected to Tom's drinking beer with Mr. Jelks in the garden evenings which isn't standard practice either but what made him really mad was the way they made fun of him. I don't make no more pretense to beauty than what you do Wilb he said to Mr. Pope but I ain't going to be laughed at. If I ain't got cleaner hocks than that slob Tom I'll go over to the boneyard and give myself up.

Mr. Pope had been a little sore himself at the giggles and easily overheard remarks that had been passed every time he appeared mounted on Ed. But he didn't see what he could do and he certainly didn't want the horse to start anything. Ed's methods were pretty direct. So he tried to rouse sympathy for Mr. Jelks' infirmity—telling Ed what a terrible inferiority complex such an eye must give the poor man and how bad it must make him feel— Yeah? said Ed.

Well it ain't anything to the way it makes me feel. The guy's so cockeyed it makes my head ache to look at him. O sure I'm sorry for him. I been thinking how I could help him. Do you think a good bat side the head might jolt that eye back into position? If you want to keep on eating at my expense said Mr. Pope firmly you'll let those two strictly alone.

This threat usually worked with Ed and having bound him over to keep the peace Mr. Pope felt easier. It was bad enough having Mrs. Pope at him to avenge fancied insults without having to worry about what Ed might do. But Ed was behaving pretty well. At least he seemed to be although there were one or two odd things. Mr. Pope noticed that when they started out for a ride now Ed kept his head turned towards the Haight garden and if Mr. Jelks and Tom were there as was usually the case there were no more snickers and jibes. Instead the two men stared menacingly at the horse and seemed to be cursing under their breath. Wonder what's the matter with them? said Mr. Pope but Ed said innocently that he couldn't imagine.

Then on weekday evenings Mr. Pope noticed that Ed usually seemed to be standing close to the hedge that separated the two gardens. Ed had the run of the place and was never tied up so there wasn't anything out of the way about that. But for some reason Mr. Jelks didn't seem to like it and one evening just as Mr. Pope drove into the yard he jumped up suddenly and threw a beer bottle at the horse.

Well of course this was too much and Mr. Pope got out of the car and went over to the hedge. Look here he said angrily you can't do that sort of thing. Ah shut your mouth snarled Mr. Jelks and he turned his back and walked towards the house but Tom grinned and said You mustn't mind Pete. He's kinda touchy about his eye and that horse of yours has spent the last week looking crosseyed at him. O come said Mr. Pope a horse can't look crosseyed. Well maybe that animal ain't a horse said Tom. We had our doubts about him. But I'm telling you mister whatever he is he can look as crosseyed as an old maid in a thunderstorm. And if you taught him that trick— Nonsense said Mr. Pope I hope I have something better to do than teach a horse how to look like your friend.

Tom's grin wasn't so genial and his eyes began to bulge. All right mister he said I'm warning you. He stared at Mr. Pope a minute and then he laughed. Hell he said I guess

we're both saying more than we meant to. Pete's a good guy—
got a heart of gold. He wants to be neighborly same as you
do. Tell you what—you come over and have some beer and
I'll get Pete to come out and apologize to your horse. Mr.
Pope said no thanks—he merely wanted it understood that
there was to be no more bottle throwing if Mr. Jelks wished
to avoid trouble with the police. So Tom said Have it your
own way mister and went back to his beer.

So Ed had sort of drifted off around the corner of the barn
and Mr. Pope went after him. As he got to the corner Ed stuck
his head around it and said Hey lookit Wilb—who's this?
And he looked crosseyed. So that's what you were doing?
said Mr. Pope. No wonder he threw the bottle and I wish
he'd hit you. You know what I told you—if there was any
monkey business you wouldn't eat. Aw Wilb said Ed I
couldn't help it. You know how it is when you're with some
guy that stammers and pretty soon you begin stammering
too? Well it's the same with this guy. When I look at him
my eyes just seem to cross of their own accord. What you
call involuntary I guess. Well you don't have to stand there
looking at him all day long said Mr. Pope. The guy fascinates
me said Ed. Anyway he said there's something funny about
those two galoots. What I mean there's lots of funny people in Mt. Kisco an' around but there's one thing they don't
any of them do—they don't any of 'em wear their city
clothes on Sunday. They'll wear things that a monkey would
blush to be seen in but you won't ever catch 'em in city
clothes. But this Jelks—you get him out on the lawn on
Sunday and what's he got on?—city clothes. It ain't natural.
I guess you're right said Mr. Pope. He don't seem to fit into
suburban life. Just the same you lay off him.

Well of course Mrs. Pope had seen the whole thing from
the window and she went right after Mr. Pope. She said O
sure he could protect his horse all right but when his wife
was insulted what did he do about it?—he did nothing that's
what he did and if he cared more for his horse than he did
for her— Mr. Pope said Don't be silly Carlotta. I don't think
it's silly said Mrs. Pope if you place your horse's welfare
before your wife's. Well said Mr. Pope Jelks threw a bottle at
Ed. When he throws a bottle at you let me know. I promise
you I'll do something about it. How like you Wilbur! said
Mrs. Pope contemptuously. And then I suppose you'll write
him a letter. So the argument went on. Though not as long as

usual for it only lasted three days because on the following Saturday Mr. Hammersley came.

This Mr. Hammersley was a pretty cold proposition because he had no weaknesses. He had a disconcerting habit of not laughing when you expected him to. At stories that would have had you or me rolling off the davenport he didn't even smile. I don't mean he wasn't polite. He showed his teeth. But to him fun was like liquor—a minor vice that was no good for the long pull.

Sunday morning Mr. Pope saddled Ed and started out for a ride. Mr. Jelks and Tom were in the Haight garden and Mrs. Pope and Mr. Hammersley were on the terrace. Mr. Pope tried to sway with nonchalant grace in the saddle as Ed clumped down the drive under this unusually heavy fire but he only felt shabby. Out on the road Ed said How you getting on with Cousin Laurence? I'm afraid said Mr. Pope that he thinks I'm rather vulgar. Well you are vulgar said Ed. Of the earth earthy—that's us Wilb. You and me. You got kind of a veneer onto you—that's the only difference between us. I expect if Cousin Laurence had his way there'd be a couple of mercy killings in the Pope family. Well I'd rather have that Jelks around than him. I could kick some sense into Jelks. But kick Cousin Laurence and you'd have to keep on kicking him and he'd just keep on snarling nobly till he died. Though that said Ed might be kind of pleasant too.

They rode up a back road and sat under a tree and Mr. Pope told Ed about the pearls. There are eighty-six pearls he said. Graduated. Wouldn't you know it? said Ed. You wouldn't catch that guy traveling around with a lot of common pearls. Graduated, hey? Pearls from educated oysters I suppose. Well they aren't cultured pearls anyway said Mr. Pope and then he had to explain the difference between cultured and natural pearls and how in both cases it was an irritation in the oyster that produced the pearl. Ed thought that if an oyster handed out a pearl every time it got irritated it might be a good idea to get some oysters and tease them. I wish Jelks was an oyster he said. I'd be wearing pearls today if he was. But look Wilbur he said has her cousin got the pearls with him?

Mr. Pope said he had. Mr. Hammersley had told them that he had brought the string because he wanted to take it into Tiffany's and have it restrung. That don't sound kosher to me said Ed. Why would *he* bother if it belongs to your wife? I mean he'd just hand it over and if the string busted he should worry. Something in that said Mr. Pope. H'm. I wonder.

So that evening after dinner when they were sitting on the terrace under the uncertain eyes of Mr. Jelks Mr. Pope said You know Laurence I don't see why you should bother to have those pearls restrung. After all it's rather up to Carlotta to see to that isn't it? Mr. Hammersley looked faintly annoyed for a minute and then he said I suppose I should be glad that you've brought that up Wilbur. It is of course the main reason why I came to see you—to clear up the misunderstanding about the pearls. What misunderstanding? said Mrs. Pope. Why as you know he said your Aunt Amelia's entire estate was left to me. There was nothing in the will— you heard it read Carlotta—which stated or even implied that there were any exceptions. You mean you're keeping them yourself? said Mrs. Pope incredulously. But good heavens Laurence Aunt Amelia told me repeatedly— I have heard you say so interrupted Mr. Hammersley and I will admit that once or twice she made a more or less vague statement to that effect to me. But after all we can only go by her intentions at the time she made her will.

O come Laurence put in Mr. Pope everybody in Carlotta's family knew she was to have those pearls. I know there was such an impression said Mr. Hammersley coldly but unfortunately it was not founded on fact. As executor of the will I have no choice— But to grab something that doesn't belong to you! interrupted Mrs. Pope bitterly. Why Laurence I never heard of such a dishonest thing! Wilbur what are you going to do about it?

Well I don't know Carlotta said Mr. Pope. If Laurence wants to be a rat I don't see how we can stop him. I suppose maybe if you can get some witnesses who heard your aunt say the pearls were to go to you— I won't have a family lawsuit interrupted Mrs. Pope and if that's all you can think of—why Wilbur I'm amazed at you! Can't you stick up for me in anything? Since Wilbur doesn't seem to be able to protect you from annoyance by those people next door I hardly think he will attempt to take the pearls by force. You mean you've got them on you? said Mr. Pope and Mr. Hammersley said Naturally. I'm taking them into town tomorrow.

Mrs. Pope looked beseechingly at Mr. Pope but he had

just caught sight of Ed's head sticking around the corner of the barn and motioning urgently for him to come. He hesitated a moment then said Excuse me and walked down off the terrace. Behind him he heard Mrs. Pope say And that's the help you get from a husband.

Hey look Wilb said Ed I just found out something. That guy Jelks does lip reading. That's why he's been staring so. All those remarks your wife thought were cracks were just him translating for Tom. Look—stay here a minute and let me walk up along the hedge. Maybe I can hear something.

So Mr. Pope waited and after a minute Ed came back. Worse than I thought he said. Just as I got there Tom says Well if he's got 'em on him what are we waiting for? And look—he's going in the house. You got to act quick Wilb. They're after those pearls.

But Mr. Pope laughed. O sure he said and I suppose they're part of a gang of international jewel thieves and pretty soon a mysterious little guy in a turban will peek out of the bedroom window and— This ain't any time to be funny said Ed. I'm not kidding. That's a valuable string of pearls and there's crooks that know how to find out about such things even in Philadelphia. I still think you've been reading too many detective stories said Mr. Pope but what do you want me to do?—have Laurence hide them somewhere in the house? Or jump in the car and take them into New York tonight? You think your cousin would believe you and let you hide them? said Ed. He'd think it was a trick to get possession. Sure maybe I do read detective stories but you listen to Old Sherlock Ed. You got to act. Like it says in the Times yesterday—your sittin' around and waiting for those guys to start something is just leaving the initiative to the enemy. You used to be pretty good with the gloves before you got soft. Go on and get all steamed up about the way Jelks is staring at your wife. Go over and sock him on the nose.

Yeah you'd like that wouldn't you? said Mr. Pope. Why not call the police? Because said Ed before the cops got here you'll be tied up in a chair and your pearls will be gone. Use some sense. Jelks has this worked out to a split second. Well said Mr. Pope hesitantly. I hope you know what you're talking about— Go on you sap said Ed. The worst you can get is a busted nose and your wife will tie it up and cry over it. You ought to be glad of a little sympathy from her the way she's been giving you the pincers lately.

So rather reluctantly Mr. Pope went out. Never having

picked a fight before he was in doubt as to just what form his remonstrance should take. But he needn't have worried. For Ed followed him and as he pushed through the hedge the horse yelled Hey you—Jelks! I'm coming over to give you a lesson in manners!

Mr. Jelks naturally assumed that it was Mr. Pope who had spoken. He got up. Mr. Pope saw that his wife and Mr. Hammersley had also risen and were looking after him in amazement. He felt pretty foolish. But he had to go on now. He tried to match the ferocity of Mr. Jelks' scowl and felt that he was doing pretty well but he knew that anything he might say would sound weak. But Mr. Jelks spoke first. Go on home you fool he said contemptuously before you get hurt.

This was just what Mr. Pope needed. He suddenly realized that he was after all good and mad at this ruffian who had been ridiculing him all these weeks. Yet he was rather startled at his capacity for vulgar behavior when he heard himself say that he'd go home when he got good and ready and was Jelks man enough to interfere with this plan? Even then though he might not have started anything if Ed who was following him closely hadn't given him a sharp nudge and driven him into Mr. Jelks' waiting arms.

For a moment the two men stood in what must have seemed to Mrs. Pope a surprisingly affectionate embrace. A closer view however would have shown that Mr. Jelks was expressing his regard by trying to throttle Mr. Pope and that Mr. Pope was responding with some very effective pokes in the torso. Then Mr. Jelks flung Mr. Pope off and attempted to kick him in the stomach. This act brought to Mr. Pope confirmation of his supicion that Mr. Jelks was not a gentleman. He leaped wildly backward fell over a chair and before he could recover Mr. Jelks hit him squarely on the bridge of the nose.

Mr. Pope thought as he fell that this was just what Ed had predicted. The blow had temporarily blinded him and as he bounced to his feet again he could do nothing but swing hopefully at the place where Mr. Jelks ought to be. He took a blow in the ribs and felt his own fist thump on something solid and then his eyes cleared and he saw that he was swinging at the empty air and that Mr. Jelks was lying flat on his back on the lawn.

Well! said Mr. Pope and looked around at Ed. The horse winked at him. Well played Mt. Kiscol he whispered. Yeah said Mr. Pope but did I—? Keep your eye on the ball said Ed sharply. For Mr. Jelks had scrambled up and was running towards the house. After him! said Ed.

Mr. Pope was still a little dazed or he would have disregarded Ed and gone back home. But as he hesitated Ed nudged him forward. What's the matter with you? said the horse. You've seized the initiative and now you want to sit down and talk about it and lose it again. You read too many newspapers said Mr. Pope feeling cautiously of his nose but he allowed himself to be herded up to the Jelks' front door.

The door was a stout iron-banded construction of oak which led directly from outdoors into the big studio. As they reached it they heard a bar dropped in place inside. Come out Jelks you coward and let me finish you off! shouted Ed. Damn it Ed shut up! said Mr. Pope. And come on home before he comes out with a gun. That guy couldn't aim a gun said Ed. Leave it to me. He backed up to the door and glancing over his shoulder to gauge his distance shouted I'm coming in Jelks! and let fly with both hind legs in a tremendous kick. The first impact of the heavy iron shoes sprung the door from the casing—the second drove it completely off its hinges and halfway across the studio and Ed whirled and having assured himself that the shrubbery hid them from Mrs. Pope's sight seized Mr. Pope's collar in his teeth and marched him into the breach.

The apparent determination with which Mr. Pope entered the studio was due entirely to Ed's final shove, but it put the finishing touch on Mr. Jelks. Mr. Pope was not the soft-muscled office worker he had supposed. Mr. Pope had bounced up after a knockdown and felled him with a blow so lightning swift that he hadn't even seen it coming. Mr. Pope had then chased him into the house and had easily kicked in a door that would have kept an elephant out. Mr. Pope was not a person to be trifled with. Mr. Jelks sat in a chair with his head in his hands.

Tom too had seen the door kicked in. He had been taking off his coat preparatory to going into action but was now prudently putting it on again.

Well Pope what do you want now? said Mr. Jelks wearily. Want? said Mr. Pope. He felt pretty good. Maybe Ed was right about this taking the initiative stuff that he got out of the papers. Even if you didn't know quite what initiative you were taking. I'll tell you what I want he said. I want you

to quit annoying me and my wife. Is that clear? If we
were annoying you why didn't you say so instead of coming
over and picking a fight? said Mr. Jelks reasonably. At least
it sounded reasonable to Mr. Pope but he knew better than
to admit it. I'm saying so now he said. Furthermore he said
you might as well give up the idea of getting those pearls.
I've laid all the information before the police and— Pearls?
said Mr. Jelks. What are you talking about? And Tom looked
at Mr. Pope and shook his head pityingly.

O don't stall said Mr. Pope. I know you could understand
what Mrs. Pope and I were saying by reading our lips and—
Brother said Mr. Jelks I can't even understand what you say
when you yell in my ear—say nothing of— He broke off as
voices came from outside and a state trooper came through
the doorway. What's wrong here? said the trooper. Hello Mr.
Pope. Your wife sent for me—

Behind the trooper were Mrs. Pope and Mr. Hammersley.
They peered fearfully then Mrs. Pope rushed in. O Wilbur!
she cried throwing her arms around her husband. O are you
all right? But Mr. Pope was in no mood to be cuddled.
Everything's under control Harvey he said to the trooper.
Just a little disagreement which has been settled satisfactori-
ly. Unless Mr. Jelks wishes to make a charge? Mr. Jelks
shook his head without looking up.

Mr. Pope began to feel sorry for him. He went over and
looked at the bruise on the side of his head. You ought to get
something on that he said. I'm sorry I hit you so hard. The
trooper also looked at the bruise then curiously at Mr. Pope.
You must have a punch like the hind leg of a mule he said
admiringly. The hind leg of a mule! said Mr. Pope thoughtfully. He bent to look more closely. Mr. Jelks made an
irritable movement and glanced up briefly. My God! Mr.
Pope exclaimed. Your eyes! They're all right!

O go away will you? said Mr. Jelks. Sure sure said Mr.
Pope. But that's funny Harvey he said in a low voice to the
trooper. He was crosseyed when I hit him. But his eyes are
as straight as mine now. Yeah? said the trooper. He put his
hand on Jelks' shoulder. Let's have a look mister he said. He
put out a hand to stop Tom who was preparing to wrap a
wet towel around Mr. Jelks' head. Mr. Jelks started angrily
to say something—then shrugged and looked up. H'm said the
trooper. Wonder if I could have a little talk with Mr. Jelks?
he said. Mr. Pope said Come on Carlotta.

Ed was slouching on three legs outside the door. Mr. Pope

caught at his halter and fell back to allow his wife and her
cousin to go on ahead. Funny thing Ed he murmured that
the marks of my knuckles on the side of Jelks' head look as
if they had been made by a horseshoe. Yeah that is funny
at that said Ed. You might have killed the guy said Mr.
Pope. In war said Ed sententiously humanitarian princi-
ples must be subordinated. The individual human life— My
lord! interrupted Mr. Pope I wish you'd skip the editorial
page just one morning. O K said Ed but it's sound sense just
the same. Like what I said about initiative. You still got it you
know. And now's the time if you want your wife to have that
jewelry. It's all in the timing Wilb. A drive on Cousin
Laurence now you've cleaned off the Jelks offensive and your
prestige is up— O quit talking like Arthur Cronkite and go
back to your stall said Mr. Pope. And quit teaching me news-
paper strategy. I've got something to say to you about this
affair but it can wait till later. Go on he said—beat it. Ed
grinned and said I go master I go. And what's more he went.

Well they went back on the terrace and sat down and
Mrs. Pope fussed over Mr. Pope in a most gratifying way
and wanted to put something on his nose which was turning
purple and she said O Wilbur—your voice when you shouted
at that Jelks man! Why I never supposed you— Skip it said
Mr. Pope I've got other matters to see to. They looked at
him inquiringly and he got up and stood over Mr. Hammersley and said Laurence don't you think you'd better hand
those pearls over to Carlotta now?

Mr. Hammersley looked up and showed his teeth and said
My dear Wilbur! I had hoped that it wouldn't be necessary
to reopen what can only be for all of us a rather unpleasant
subject. Surely I explained— So you did said Mr. Pope.
And you're pretty sure Carlotta can't get the pearls by due
process of law. You wouldn't mind such a lawsuit either.
You could make it look like a grab and it wouldn't hurt your
standing in Philadelphia. But suppose it comes out in another way. Suppose you've got in a fight with me and been
beaten up—not because we wanted the pearls but because
we thought you were a skunk. We acknowledge your legal
right to the pearls but we knock the stuffing out of you. And
then tell everybody why—hey?

Mrs. Pope put her hand on his arm. Really Wilbur she
said hesitantly I don't think this is the way— Shut up said
Mr. Pope. Now Laurence?

Mr. Hammersley was apparently quite cool but there was a

faint dew on his forehead. And suppose he said that you found yourself incapable of—as you put it—knocking the stuffing out of me? Frankly said Mr. Pope I hadn't thought of that. Because frankly it isn't possible. You saw what happened to Jelks. He was crosseyed and I knocked his eyes straight. It is within the bounds of possibility Laurence that I might knock you cockeyed.

Then suddenly he reached down and seized Mr. Hammersley by the necktie and jerked him out of his chair. Come on he said hand them over. They kind of eyed each other for a minute and then Mr. Hammersley reached slowly into his inside pocket and took out a case which he dropped on the table. He shook Mr. Pope's hand from his tie and turned away but Mr. Pope called him back. Sit down there said Mr. Pope and write out an acknowledgment that the pearls belong to Carlotta and that you are carrying out her Aunt Amelia's wishes and so on. And we'll get it witnessed. Harvey's still over at Jelks' Carlotta. Run over and get him.

By the time Mr. Hammersley had finished writing Mrs. Pope had returned with the trooper. Mr. Jelks accompanied them but although Mr. Pope was surprised at this he felt that another witness would do no harm so he asked them both to sign. Nathan Stanner? he said looking at the signatures. I've heard that name somewhere. But your name is Jelks. That's what I thought Mr. Pope said the trooper with a grin. Until I got a look at him without his squint. You know it's funny how a little thing like that will change a guy's looks. I've seen him around here a dozen times and never thought anything about him. You know who he is? Nathan Stanner—wanted for income tax evasion. That crosseyed stuff was his disguise you might say. Like that guy used to be in the movies—Ben Turpin. Then I didn't knock his eye straight after all? said Mr. Pope. Hell no! burst out Mr. Jelks. It hurt too much to keep 'em crossed after you hit me. H'm said Mr. Pope thoughtfully. Well look after your pearls Carlotta. So long Harvey. If you'll excuse me—

He went down to the barn. Look here Ed he said those fellows were no more jewel thieves than I am. They weren't lip reading. Most of that staring Jelks did was just to show people he was crosseyed. You don't say? said Ed. That's funny now isn't it? Very funny said Mr. Pope. Yeah said Ed I suppose you think I made the whole thing up? Well I tell you Wilbur—I expect I could have misunderstood what I heard 'em say. But honest— Don't perjure yourself said

Mr. Pope. But I'll just ask you to look what you got me into. I won't be able to show my face for a week.

Ed stamped impatiently. O what you bellyachin' about? he said. Your wife thinks you're a hero don't she? You got her the pearls didn't you? My gosh isn't that worth a sock in the nose? Well said Mr. Pope thoughtfully maybe you're right Ed—we'll say no more about it. Just as you say said the horse. Only I was hoping it had taught you a lesson. It's like I said about the initiative. Once you lose it the other side's got you by the whiskers. You must therefore constantly maintain it—by action—by surprise attacks even though they be of little tactical value. One sees evidences in the current situation in the Near East—

Mr. Pope groaned and going to the harness closet brought out a whiskey bottle. Look Ed he said if you'll shut up—and keep shut—I'll split this with you. That's the only smart word you've said today said Ed. Pass it over Wilb. This here strategy is dry work.

Just a Song at Twilight

The Popes had had new cooks every month or so but Carrie was the first good one they had ever had. Her soups were collectors' items and her soufflés were so light that they would float in the bathtub. But she was not contented. She'd always lived in the city and she was lonesome in Mt. Kisco. She had no gentleman callers at all. Though I think the fault was with Carrie rather than with Mt. Kisco. The way to a man's heart may be through his stomach but the way to his stomach is through his face and if he won't face you in the first place you haven't much chance of getting him to try your cooking. So Carrie began to talk about leaving.

So Mrs. Pope was talking about it one evening. O dear she said if Carrie leaves I guess we'll just have to give up the house and take an apartment in town. Well Mr. Pope did not want to leave Mt. Kisco for many reasons and one of them was that he wouldn't be able to keep his horse Ed in the city. Of course Mrs. Pope didn't know that Ed could talk and she was always at Mr. Pope to get rid of him because he was such an awful looking horse. And indeed Ed was not handsome. But he was darned good company and Mr. Pope was much attached to him. So he began to depict the advantages of Mt. Kisco. He ranged freely among the adjectives and was just getting going good when somewhere out in the night a hoarse voice began to sing:

> "O my darling Carrie!
> The girl I'm going to marry!
> Every evening just at eight,
> Standing by the garden gate—"

Good heavens said Mrs. Pope is that Carrie singing? Not unless her voice is changing said Mr. Pope. I've heard her singing at her work.

"O what bliss
for just one kiss
from Car-rie!"

"O what bliss
For just one kiss
From Ca-a-arriel"

The voice ended with a roar. Good Lord! said Mr. Pope
I'd better go see.

The kitchen was dark and he went through it and out into
the garden. There seemed to be nobody there. Then a voice
from an upper window said That was right pretty Mr.—I
guess I don't know your name. Mr. Pope looked up. Is that
you Carrie? he said. O excuse me Mr. Pope said Carrie
with a heavy giggle. I thought you was him. Him? said Mr.
Pope. Who? I don't know said Carrie.

We don't seem to be getting anywhere said Mr. Pope. That
wasn't you singing was it? Me? said Carrie. Lord no sir I can't
even carry a tune. This fellow could carry one all right said
Mr. Pope though I don't know where he carried it to. He
seems to have disappeared. Yes sir said the cook I guess he
heard you come out. She giggled again. I kind of thought she
said that he was—well kind of serenading me like. I see said
Mr. Pope. An anonymous admirer.

So he went in and told Mrs. Pope. Heavens! she said do
you think this is to be a regular feature? I don't think so said
Mr. Pope. No human throat could stand the strain. But if
it makes Carrie happy! O if it makes her contented said Mrs.
Pope I'd accept a fife and drum corps.

Well before going to bed Mr. Pope went out to say good
night to Ed. He kept a bottle in the barn and he and Ed
usually had a nightcap together. Well Wilb said the horse
how did you enjoy the concert? O so you listened to that too?
said Mr. Pope. Listened to it! said Ed. Hell I gave it! You
what? said Mr. Pope. Gave it said Ed. You see Wilbur that
Carrie—she's kind of starved for romance the way I figure
it. And when I see somebody that's unhappy—well I have to
try to make things a little easier for them. You take a funny
way to do it said Mr. Pope. I suppose it seems funny to you
said Ed seeing you ain't got a fine natural baritone like I
have. Never had a lesson in my life—would you believe it?

Look Ed said Mr. Pope let's not go into what I think of
your voice. What surprises me is the age of your repertoire.
That Carrie song is a moss-back. When you've lived around
stables as long as I have said Ed you'll know a lot of songs.
Some of 'em ain't exactly the kind you sing to ladies though.

Listen Wilb—jever hear this one? It goes Stampee stampoodle stianti go foodle— Yes interrupted Mr. Pope I know it and I'm surprised at you Ed. I'm going to bed. And no lullabies please.

Well the next evening Ed serenaded Carrie again. *Stars of the summer night* crashed in a blitzkrieg on the eardrums of the Popes as they sat at bridge with the Hoveys. Really we can't have this said Mrs. Pope. Wilbur go send that person away. So Mr. Pope went out and found Ed among the syringas under Carrie's window. She sleeps! Ed roared. My lady sleeps! Like hell she does said Mr. Pope. Through that hullabaloo! Well said Ed the guy that wrote the song didn't really expect her to sleep or he wouldn't have sung it. Psst! There she is!

A wide shape appeared at the window and something was tossed out and fell on the grass. It's a rose whispered Ed. Pick it up for me will you? Mr. Pope hesitated but Carrie could not possibly recognize him in the darkness so he stepped out from the bushes and retrieved the rose. My beloved! said Ed tenderly. I shall always cherish this flower next my heart. Carrie giggled. *O you* she said. Wait she said. I'll be down. No no said Ed I cannot reveal myself to you. Not yet. O I guess you can said Carrie. I've got half of a nice cherry pie for you. Wait. She vanished.

I've got to go back in Mr. Pope said to Ed. Now be careful. We don't want to lose Carrie. Neither do I want to lose her said Ed. Anybody that passes out pies.

Well the next day was Saturday and Ed and Mr. Pope went for a ride. They never rode very far. Today as usual they got as far as the nearest tavern where they had some beer and then they found a shady place and sat down and talked. How did you come out with Carrie? asked Mr. Pope. O I got the pie said Ed. Yeah. She came out on the back porch with it and I says Hey don't come any farther. I don't want you to recognize me. I've got a special reason I says and if you'll sit down I'll tell you about it. So she sat down in her rocker and I come up closer to her behind all that woodbine and then I told her that I was a friend of yours that came to the house regular and that I had sort of fallen for her but I didn't want her to know who I was yet because it would be embarrassing for both of us—her waiting on me and us pretending not to know each other and so on. But I said I'd like to serenade her and talk to her and then I said when the time was ripe I'd disclose myself. And I left it sort of vague what would happen after that. I should think so! said Mr. Pope.

Well I don't know said Ed. You see how it'll work don't you? I'll come around and give her a sort of romantic interest in life and she won't talk any more about leaving. And when you have company she'll make a special effort because she'll think maybe it's me. I expect she'll pick on Bill Wesson said Mr. Pope. He's got a voice something like yours. She left the pie out for me when she went in said Ed. 'Twasn't exactly a balanced meal with your Bourbon she poured out for me to wash it down with but it set like a feather.

Well I guess it was the next Sunday the Wessons came to dinner. They all had a few drinks and then Mr. Wesson went in to the piano. He had kind of a bass voice. His low notes sounded like a bus going over a bridge. He struck a chord and rumbled into *Asleep in the Deep*.

O Judas! said Mr. Pope and he pulled his chair around so that he could see into the living-room window. After a minute Carrie came and stood in the doorway gazing at the singer with heavy rapture. Beware! So beware! thundered Mr. Wesson. It was a better voice than Ed's but had the same quality. That was lovely Mr. Wesson said Carrie. Why thank you Carrie I'm glad you liked it said Mr. Wesson. Carrie came closer. Look Mr. Wesson she said the folks are all outside. Aren't you—well honest now aren't you the one? The *one?* said Mr. Wesson. I don't get you Carrie. Well you—you *could* Mr. Wesson said Carrie coyly. Then she said Shucks you don't have to be afraid of me. I won't give you away.

Well I don't know what Mr. Wesson had been up to but he turned pale. I—I don't know what you mean he said. And then Mr. Pope who had been practically cataleptic with amusement and horror came and stuck his head in the window. Oughtn't you to be looking after the dinner Carrie? he said. And Carrie squawked and left.

So they had dinner and nothing happened except that everybody noticed the sheep's eyes that Carrie served with every dish to Mr. Wesson and Mrs. Wesson said Bill seems to have been turning the old charm on again. But after the Wessons had gone Mrs. Pope told Mr. Pope that Carrie had given notice. Notice! said Mr. Pope why I thought she just decided that she wasn't lonesome any more. Well she's changed again said Mrs. Pope.

Well that's a fine thing! said Mr. Pope. But later he got the explanation from Ed. She thinks I'm that Wesson guy said the horse. And she thinks if she gets another job with people who don't know me I won't be afraid to come around and see her.

So Ed's scheme to keep Carrie had backfired. He felt pretty low. But there was one thing about Ed—he never gave up hope and the day Carrie left he overheard her give the expressman the address to which she wanted her trunk sent. Ed knew the house for the Witherspoons who were friends of the Popes had lived there. The present tenant was a Mr. O'Malley. So the next night which was a Wednesday he slipped his halter and at 3 A.M. he was in the O'Malley's back garden and at 3:02 he burst into *O my darling Carrie.*

But instead of singing *Every evening just at eight* he changed the lines and sang—

Monday evening just at nine
Meet me where the grapevines twine.

For there was a grape arbor at the lower end of the garden. He sang those lines twice over and then he trotted off home. Over his shoulder he could see lights springing up in the house.

So Friday morning at two he sang *O Promise Me* in the O'Malleys' garden and Saturday morning at four he sang *In the Gloaming* and Sunday at 1:45 he sang *Juanita* and was struck on the rump by a brick thrown by the enraged O'Malley. And on Monday evening at nine he was concealed behind the grape arbor. Presently through the glimmering scented dusk came Carrie. Psst! Mr. Wesson! Carrie whispered. I'm behind the arbor said Ed. Well come out where I can see you said Carrie. I want to talk to you. She didn't seem in a very good humor. Listen said Ed I'm not coming out because I don't want you to know who I am yet. You see I know the O'Malleys just as well as I do the Popes. But I know who you are said Carrie You're— No interrupted Ed I'm not Wesson and how you could ever mistake his voice for mine I don't know.

Look here said Carrie you've got to stop this singing. Waking everybody up like you've been doing! Why I'm sorry if

I've bothered the folks said Ed. But you know how it is—when I get feeling romantic it don't matter what time of night it is. I just have to pour my soul out in song. Well you'd better pour it out somewhere else said Carrie. Land sakes! When I come here I thought you'd quit being afraid to show yourself. But all you want to do is sit out and sing like a bird in a bush. O I like your singing all right but I like my job better and this O'Malley ain't a softy like that Mr. Pope. He come out in the kitchen this morning and he said if it happened again out I go.

Ed gave a snort. The man's dead to romance he said. Glorious summer night and a full moon and a mysterious singer in the garden. What more could the guy want? He could maybe want to sleep said Carrie. Anyway like it is now all I know about you is you got a voice and an appetite. Now I want you to promise me you won't do any more serenading.

There isn't hardly anything I wouldn't promise you Carrie said Ed but that's the one thing I can't. The song is in my heart and when it seeks expression I cannot deny it. It just comes bubbling out of me like beer out of a bottle. You just want to lose me my job then said Carrie. Well said Ed you can always go back to the Popes. I heard them talking about you only the other day, and wishing you'd come back.

Well Ed was so pleased with himself that he told Mr. Pope all about it. O'Malley's sore all right he said and I think a couple more good rousing serenades will do the trick and he'll fire her. Then she won't dast go anywhere else, and she'll have to come back here. But Mr. Pope said No. You've done enough Ed he said. You're pointed for trouble. This O'Malley is president of some municipal board or other. He's in politics. You know what that means. Tough guy eh? said Ed. You mean he might plant somebody in the rhododendrons with a cannon? You can't knock off a guy just because you don't like his voice. But to make things certain Mr. Pope bought a new halter Ed couldn't slip out of and tied him securely in his stall.

At least he thought he tied him securely. But about two next morning something awoke him. He went to the window and saw movement in the shadows by the stable. Mr. Pope dressed and went out. Ed's stall was empty and the halter rope gnawed in two. He got in his car and drove over towards the O'Malleys'. The darned old fool he said if I don't round him up he'll get his silly hide full of buckshot. He was really worried.

Mr. Pope knew the layout of the O'Malley grounds. He drove down a back road and stopped and got out. When he had stumbled across two fields he was behind the hedge at the foot of the O'Malley garden. And just too late. A hoarse voice blasted the night. *She was only a bird in a gilded cage* . . .

Mr. Pope swore and scrambled through the hedge. Ed! he said. Come out of there you fool! The song broke off and Ed came trotting up. Hi Wilb he whispered. Glad you came. This is better with two voices. Suppose you could take the tenor? But before Mr. Pope could answer flashlights flickered through the leaves and a voice said You take the other side Joe. We got him cornered.

Quick Wilb! said Ed. Back through the hedge and lie low. I'll fox 'em. And as Mr. Pope obeyed he moved down along the hedge making a good deal of noise. Mr. Pope saw the flashlights converge to his right and then there was an exclamation and another voice said Hey O'Malley we caught a horse. Got a broken halter. Well I don't know how he got here said O'Malley but that wasn't any horse singing. The fellow must be right here. He can't get away except across the field. Go outside Canby and watch if he breaks through the hedge.

Ed had wandered off with the intention of creating a diversion by bursting into song on the other side of the house. But Mr. Pope didn't know that and fearing to be cut off he bolted. In the open field the flashlights picked him up. He stopped running and walked slowly back.

You can take those lights out of my eyes he said. I'm only looking for my horse. All right boys said O'Malley. I know him. You're Wilbur Pope aren't you? And may I ask what the hell you are doing serenading my cook? I don't know anything about your cook said Mr. Pope. My horse got away tonight and a fellow told me he saw him up in this field so I came up after him. So *you* say said O'Malley. But I guess we've got you Mr. Pope. We were laying for you tonight. If you hear some one singing and you go out and catch a man running away and there isn't anybody else in the garden you're pretty sure you've got the right man.

At that moment another man came up leading Ed. Here's my horse now said Mr. Pope. You can see he's not saddled for riding. You could ride him bareback said O'Malley. I guess you'd better come in the house Mr. Pope and we'll have a talk with the cops. Canby give Lieutenant Payson a ring will you?

The interrogation that followed was minute. Mrs. O'Malley who was a pretty dark-eyed girl was present and seemed to find it amusing but O'Malley was dead serious. Finally Carrie was brought down. She admitted that she had worked for the Popes—that she had been serenaded while there. Did it ever occur to you said O'Malley that it might be Mr. Pope who was doing the so-called singing? I protest against these idiotic questions O'Malley said Mr. Pope. You're making a fool of yourself. Somebody's making a fool of himself said O'Malley but it's not me. Answer please Carrie. Why no sir Carrie said but— But what? said O'Malley You say you never saw the singer? Well sir I did once said Carrie and giggled. Just sort of faintly when he—when he picked up a rose I threw him. A rose! murmured Mrs. O'Malley. Did he look like Mr. Pope? asked O'Malley. Why sir now you speak of it said Carrie he did—sort of. Yes sir it could have been him. Only— Only what? said O'Malley Well said Carrie it wasn't his voice. Disguised said O'Malley I thought that all the time. No human could have a natural voice like that.

The bell rang at this point and two state troopers were shown in. Following them came Joe rubbing his arm. The horse got away Mr. O'Malley he said. He bit me in the arm. Well he'll find his way home I daresay said O'Malley. Sit down boys he said to the troopers. Then he turned to Mr. Pope. I don't want to be too hard on you he said. Maybe we haven't a charge strong enough to hold you on but I'm convinced you're the man and whether we can hold you or not the newspapers—well you know what they'd do to you. So I'm giving you a choice. Either I turn you over to these boys here or you'll write out a full statement admitting the singing and all the rest of it and—

Just a minute! said Mr. Pope jumping up. I've told you the exact truth O'Malley. I came after my horse. I haven't been singing to your cook or in your garden. You've called me a liar and tried to make me out a lunatic. I know you're sore and I don't blame you. But I think you are a vindictive rat and before I'd sign—

Suddenly through the window came a dreadful raucous voice.

"Pale hands I loved
Besides the Shalimar-har . . ."

For a moment they sat paralyzed. Then the entire room rose and flung itself at the door.

Mr. Pope had waited on the porch and presently they trooped back to him. With the help of the state police they had combed the garden but had found nothing—nothing but a flock of mosquitoes and Ed who was peacefully cropping the grass beside the drive. I apologize Pope said O'Malley heavily. I—what can I say? This thing has got me nuts. It certainly has said Mr. Pope. I just hope the newspapers you mentioned don't get hold of it. They'll ride me plenty said O'Malley. I'll do anything Pope— Then keep your mouth shut about it said Mr. Pope. I don't want anything.—Yes what is it Carrie? he said as the cook came up to him.

Well Mr. Pope said Carrie I guess I'd like to come back if you and Mrs. Pope'll have me. She turned to O'Malley. You'll excuse me sir but I have to say it. Mr. Pope's a nice man. And you ain't treated him like a gentleman. I don't like to stay in a house where folks act that way. O'Malley shrugged and walked away. Mr. Pope grinned. Why Carrie he said we'll be glad to have you. You call up Mrs. Pope tomorrow. He went down the steps and catching hold of Ed's halter jumped on his back and trotted off down the drive. They sang part songs all the way home.

Ed Takes the Brush in His Teeth

This Wilbur Pope had a lot of things to be thankful for. He had a nice house in Mt. Kisco, and he had a good job as an architect with the firm of Lamson, Camphire, Leatherbee & Wallet, and he had a beautiful wife. I know some people consider this last item a liability rather than an asset, but Mr. Pope did not feel that way about it. And then he had his horse, Ed, on whom he used to ride around the country weekends.

Of course like everybody else he had his tribulations. Many of his friends thought that Ed was one of these, and indeed Ed did look a good deal like a tribulation. Particularly when he looked at you down his long bony nose with that sardonic eye. You certainly would never have taken him for a saddle horse. He had thick ankles, a ewe neck, and a general appearance of having been put together by an inferior workman from odds and ends left over from the manufacture of various other animals. But Mr. Pope was very fond of him.

Among Mr. Pope's tribulations Mrs. Pope's relatives had a very high rating. There were rafts of them, and one or another was always coming to New York for a week or two of shopping and mild debauchery, and of course they couldn't leave without seeing dear Carlotta. "Seeing Carlotta" however was pretty elastically interpreted. It usually meant coming out to visit for from a week to—in extreme cases—six months. It was Cousin Edith Manley who had once stayed six months.

Now Mr. Pope didn't dislike Cousin Edith, but six months is too much of anybody's cousin, and when Mrs. Pope informed him one evening on his return from the city that she had invited Cousin Edith to come out for a week or two, he just blew up.

Mrs. Pope listened to him fizzle and pop until he ran down, and then she said quietly: "Yes, darling. I know it's

*"I suppose you used a brush?" "Yeah, held it in my teeth . . .
a different technique from the one I used before."*

a nuisance, but we can't help it. It would be just too mean not to ask her this time. You see, this last winter she met Harmon Copley somewhere—"

"Harmon Copley, the art dealer?"

"Yes. And he said that if she'd bring some of her things to New York he'd come look at them, and if he liked them he'd give her a show at his gallery."

"He must be crazy," said Mr. Pope.

"He was probably just being polite. But anyway she's come, and she's been trying to find a studio in the city where she can display her paintings, and where she could do a little work on some of them before she shows them to him. She said some of them needed fixing up a little."

"I'll say they do!" said Mr. Pope. "A couple of nice coats of white paint would be the most satisfactory alteration." He looked gloomily at Mrs. Pope. "And so?"

"Well, darling, you know you can't get a hall bedroom in New York nowadays, much less a studio. And you see, too, Mr. Copley lives only about five miles from here; he could easily drive over. It did seem such a pity when she feels it's her big chance. And after all it won't be for long, and she can work out in the barn so she won't be messing the house up with her paints. Those double doors face the north, and if you throw them open it will make a perfect studio."

"Maybe we could bed her down in the box stall," said Mr. Pope, "and then she wouldn't have to come into the house at all. Lord, it's going to be tough on Ed."

Mrs. Pope sniffed. "I think consideration of Cousin Edith comes before that of your mouldy old horse." She was always a little acid where Ed was concerned. "After all, she's my own cousin."

"Well, I wouldn't brag about it," said Mr. Pope. "And I suppose you're going to have me hang those two revolting daubs she gave you last time she was here in the living room."

"We'll have to; it's only decent," Mrs. Pope said. "And they're not so awful. That one she did in Rockport of the sea—"

"I know," he said. "I suppose it must be good—at least it always makes me seasick when I look at it." He sighed. "Oh well, I always know I'm licked when Be Kind to Relatives Week comes around. There's one consolation. When Copley gets a look at the things, the party will be over—and quick!"

After dinner Mr. Pope went out to talk it all over with Ed.

"Who's she?" Ed asked, when Mr. Pope told him that Cousin Edith was coming.

"An artist," Mr. Pope said. "She was before your time here. She'll probably be after your time, too, for she never leaves until she's put out." And then he told Ed that Cousin Edith was going to paint in the stable.

Ed was indignant. "It's an outrage!" he exclaimed. "It's an invasion of my private rights under the Constitution. You can't do this to me, Wilb."

"It can't be helped, Ed," Mr. Pope said. "You see—"

"Can't be helped—can't be helped!" the horse interrupted furiously. "There ain't anything but can be helped if it ain't happened yet. Write her you got smallpox. Tell her there's mice in the stable. There is, you know."

Mr. Pope shook his head. "There's one thing I'll say for Cousin Edith. She would allow neither mice nor germs, neither rats, lions, nor centipedes, to stand between her and the practice of what she calls Art. No, Ed, you'll just have to put up with it."

"Yeah? Well, I ain't going to. How would your wife like it if I was to invite one of *my* cousins here and stable him in *her* living room? It's just the same thing." His voice dropped to a pleading note. "Ain't you got any respect for the sanctity of the home? This ain't any marble palace, God wot, but it's the best you've seen fit to give me, and after I got reconciled to living in such a dump—well, I'm fond of the place, Wilb. It's my little home . . . humble . . . dirty . . . full of mice—but still, such as it is, my lowly cot, my refuge from the busy world. I'm happy here, Wilb, with all my little possessions about me. With the bin full of oats and some hay to sleep on. It's all I've got, Wilb. And you'd bring a female into it!"

Mr. Pope grinned unsympathetically. "I expect it'll brighten up the old place quite a lot. You ought to thank me—bringing Art into the Home! Your drab walls hung with rich paintings—it'll do wonders for your cultural development. You'll probably become a connoisseur."

"I'll probably become a squeaking lunatic," said Ed.

"Now, now, Cousin Edith isn't a professional artist," Mr. Pope said. "I mean, she's never sold anything, except maybe to relatives."

"I've seen 'em," Ed said. "Up north of Boston, miles of easels along the shore, and a Cousin Edith behind every one in arty clothes, peckin' away at a six by six canvas board. And when it rains—settin' up an old bottle and a couple wilted cabbages in front of a Chinese screen."

"Well, what of it if they enjoy it?" said Mr. Pope. "Anyway, she's coming, and I expect you to behave yourself. I promise I'll get rid of her as soon as I can."

But this was mere whistling in the dark on Mr. Pope's part. Cousin Edith may have been short on talent, but she was long on enthusiasm, and she was enthusiastic about the stable. She spent the first day uncrating pictures and hanging them, and when Mr. Pope came home that evening and had greeted her, she insisted on taking him right out to see what she had done. She was a short woman in her late forties, inclining to double chins and coyness, and she took him by the hand and dragged him out to the stable. "There! Would you have believed that this old place could have been made so charming?"

Mr. Pope gasped. The paintings he had expected, but not the lengths of tattered brocade and silk that draped and hid all familiar objects, even the lawnmower in the corner. Odds and ends of discarded furniture had been hauled down from the hay loft and adapted. "That old chair," said Cousin Edith, "it was an awful old wreck, but throw a bit of stuff over it and it becomes a royal throne!" She bugged her eyes at him triumphantly.

"Yes," said Mr. Pope. "Er . . . yes." He pulled himself together. "Quite regal. You've done wonders with this old place, Cousin Edith."

"Oh, I saw its possibilities at once. The artistic eye, you know! I saw it as a challenge, a definite challenge."

"And you've met it with a fearf—I mean, a fearlessness which astounds me," he returned. His eye slid round cautiously towards Ed's stall, and again he gasped. For the horse's hindquarters were dimly visible between the folds of long flowered cretonne curtains which had been tacked up on each side of the stall.

Cousin Edith laughed delightedly. "Isn't that cute?"

"No one but you, Cousin Edith," he said, "could have thought up such a refinement. And how are you and Ed getting along?"

"Oh, beautifully! He's such a dear, Wilbur! He stamped and snorted a good deal when I was putting them up, but I went right in and explained to him, and he quieted right down."

"I don't keep him tied, you know," Mr. Pope said. "He has the run of the place and he's in and out a lot. I hope," he said, raising his voice, "that he won't knock over any of your things. I should have to beat him if he did."

Later, when Cousin Edith was in the house, Mr. Pope came back.

Ed came out of his stall. "Hell and fury, Wilb," he said, "look at them damn curtains! I don't feel respectable going in and out of this place. First thing you know she'll be sprayin' me with one of them little perfumery atomizers."

"Not a bad idea," Mr. Pope said. "But I'm afraid the cost would be prohibitive. She'd have to use a whale of a lot to get any results."

"Very funny," said Ed. "Ver-ee funny! All right, if you won't do anything I'm going to take measures myself."

"No rough stuff," Mr. Pope warned him.

"No, no," said Ed. "You know me, Wilb. The subtle touch, the iron hoof in the velvet shoe, eh? Leave it to me."

"No!" said Mr. Pope firmly. "I'm with you on this, Ed, but if there's any monkey business Carlotta will side with Cousin Edith, and we'll be a lot worse off then, let me tell you."

"O K," said Ed resignedly. "Ooooo K. Kindly step aside; I wish to return to my boudoir." He clumped off and disappeared between the cretonne curtains.

During the next few days Mr. Pope was gratified to find that Ed was behaving with unusual discretion. Cousin Edith spent most of the daylight hours in the stable, touching up and repainting parts of her pictures in preparation for the inspection by Mr. Copley. She reported that Ed was a much more satisfactory companion than many humans with whom she had shared studios. "He's as quiet as a mouse," she said. "And you know, he seems as if he were really interested in what I'm doing. He often comes up and looks over my shoulder—sometimes for an hour at a time. Do you suppose animals are interested in art? No, really—I mean, of course they wouldn't understand, but they can see pictures, and maybe they look like real scenes to them."

Ed explained, when Mr. Pope asked him about this, that he was making a virtue of necessity. "You won't let me kick her through the roof, so I got to do something, don't I? I might as well learn how these artists work. I might want to take it up myself some time. And you know, Wilb, it's kind of fascinating trying to figure out what she's doing. Like these here puzzles. She paints in something looks like it might be a man with a fishpole, and you wonder about it, and then she puts some green dabs around it and you know it's a tree. Take that picture she's got of a herd of elephants standin' on the seashore looking off into the sunset—"

"She hasn't got any picture of elephants," said Mr. Pope.

"She sure has. That one that hung over your old work bench, remember?"

"That's a group of fish houses that she painted down around Gloucester one year," Mr. Pope said.

"Fish houses! Well, they sure look like elephants to me. They're that same putty color. That just shows you how art can fool you, don't it? Yeah, I begin to see why folks are so interested in it—it's kind of a guessing game, hey?"

Mr. Pope said: "All Cousin Edith's houses are that putty color. I guess that's one of her trade secrets—how she always manages to make them look so grey and mushy. Though actually I think it's because she's so undecided about everything. She probably can't ever make up her mind what color it looks like."

"I can see there's a lot to this art business," Ed said. "When's the guy coming to look at the stuff?"

"She says she'll be ready for him next week. And then, thank heaven, we'll be rid of her. He'll tell her they're no good and she'll pack up and go."

"I ain't so sure," said Ed. "There's more to this art business than just painting something that looks like something. Of course I ain't a dealer, but dealers want to handle stuff that other folks like to look at, and I kind of like some of these things, Wilb. Take that one of the three zombies sittin' around the stone table in the graveyard at midnight—"

"Zombies!" Mr. Pope exclaimed.

"Well, maybe they're ghouls dissectin' a corpse. I ain't up on the supernatural."

"You ass, that's a tea party. Three women sitting around a tea table on a lawn."

"Yeah?" said Ed. "Well, that just shows you. I bet this griper'll take the whole lot. And she'll have to stay here all summer to paint him some more."

"Well, that would suit you, wouldn't it? You're such pals."

They were sitting under a tree by the roadside and between them was a paper bag containing six empty beer bottles. Ed got up. "Come on," he said coldly. "Let's take the empties back."

"What's the matter with you?" Mr. Pope demanded.

"Look, Wilb," said the horse slowly. "I'm laying off this dame because you want me to. I got to get a little fun out of it. But if I had my way—"

"All right, all right," said Mr. Pope. "But you just let nature take its course. Nature can lick art any day in the week. I assure you that in a week Cousin Edith will be only an unhappy memory."

Well of course she wasn't—not in a week, or two weeks. She repainted nearly every canvas she had brought with her —some of them several times. In an effort to hasten things the Popes, dragged out to look at them for the fiftieth time, tried to discourage further alterations. They were lovely, they said, just as they were.

But Cousin Edith only smiled. "Nothing short of perfection, you know—that is the artist's motto. I couldn't think of letting Mr. Copley see them until I'm quite satisfied." She sighed. "Art is long, my dears!"

It was awfully long-winded, Mr. Pope thought. His evenings were filled with it. But what did he have to complain about? Mrs. Pope wanted to know. He didn't have to listen to it all day too.

"But you don't really think Copley will come over here, do you?" he said one evening.

"He will, Wilbur. Whenever she's ready. She got him to promise. She called him up today. Oh, don't ask me why! I suppose those people don't want ever to miss a bet. She might be good—he doesn't know."

"Well, that will settle it," Mr. Pope said.

"Yes, I suppose so. But—oh, Wilbur!" she exclaimed. "You don't suppose he might—he might *like* them?"

Mr. Pope laughed. "And she'd want to stay the rest of the summer to paint more? Not a chance. I know you see some queer things in the galleries nowadays, but they're not just niddling, just completely gutless. Like these. You know what I mean?"

"Yes, of course. Oh darling, won't it be nice not to have everything smell of turpentine again?"

"That's one way of putting it," said Mr. Pope.

But at last the great day came. Cousin Edith had phoned Mr. Copley and he had promised to drive over Sunday morning. She spent Saturday morning flying from one painting to another, brush in hand, putting a dab here and a dab there.

"They'll still be pretty wet," she said, "but that doesn't matter."

On Saturday afternoon Mr. Pope and Ed went for a ride, and when they got back Cousin Edith had gone into the house. When Ed's saddle and bridle had been taken off and hung up, he clumped over and stood in front of a large picture on the easel. Mr. Pope started to close the big doors for the night, but Ed said: "Wait a minute. You know, Wilb, this picture's real pretty."

Mr. Pope came and stood beside him. The painting showed wharves, and a cove with fishing boats. There was too much of everything in it—too many wharf timbers, too many stiff little sailboats sitting on too many stiff little waves, too many cotton wool clouds surrounding a jaundiced sun. In spite of its stiffness, Cousin Edith's indecision was apparent in every brush stroke. Mr. Pope sighed. "It's too bad, in a way. She tries so hard, and it's so damned awful!"

"I don't agree with you," said Ed. "You're just saying that because it's what some of your high-toned artist friends would say. These here are nice simple pictures, the kind that ordinary folks like. And that's what worries me." He looked around. "This guy, Wilb, when he sees these pictures—maybe he won't like 'em himself, but bein' a salesman, it's more important to him what other folks like. And it ain't artists that buys pictures. He's going to realize that this is just the stuff for some of these nouveau riches like it might be myself if I made a lot of money and wanted to fix up a house. This is the Century of the Common Man, ain't it? Well, it's the common man that's getting the dough, and he's going to buy things with it."

"Maybe. But how are you so sure you know what the common man wants?"

"Because I know him," said Ed. "I've known some of the commonest men you ever saw. Oh, I don't mean you, Wilb; you're the kind of superior useless type that's headed for the ash heap. My guess is, this guy buys the whole lot of these pictures. And you know what that means."

Mr. Pope said yes, he did. "Cousin Edith would stay on here painting until cold weather. But you're needlessly alarmed, Ed. I know the kind of stuff these fellows handle, and I assure you it isn't this."

"All right, all right," said Ed crossly. "That's you all over, Wilb—papa knows best. Well, you just wait. Let's see what papa will do when he finds he's got Cousin Edith on his hands for the rest of the summer. Don't say I didn't warn you."

Cousin Edith was always astir much too early Sunday mornings, but on this one she outdid herself. At eight-thirty she rapped on the Popes' door. "Come on, children," she called. "Get up, you sleepy-heads. Time to stump the experts."

Mr. Pope moaned, then he sat up. "This is outrageous!" he said.

Mrs. Pope smiled wryly. "Never mind, darling. It's the last day."

At breakfast and during the hour or two before Mr. Copley appeared, Cousin Edith's nervousness took the form of an exaggerated fluttery coyness. Probably only the Popes' certainty of an early release saved her from being quietly lynched. But Mr. Copley came at last.

He was a large man, got up for the part of country gentleman in tweeds and a pipe. He was polite but bored, and obviously anxious to get it over with. It was plain after his first glance at Cousin Edith that he expected nothing, and this reassured the Popes. They went at once to the stable.

The stable was dark. While the others waited Mr. Pope crossed to the big doors and flung them open. Then instead of turning back, he stood for a moment looking out. For much as he wanted to get rid of Cousin Edith he felt sure that Copley's verdict would be swift and politely devastating, and he didn't want to see the disappointment on her face.

But what he heard made him swing round. Copley said: "By Jove!" in an amazed tone, and at the same moment Cousin Edith's voice was raised in a low wail: "Oh, my lovely pictures!" Then there was a sort of gurgle, and a soft thump. And he saw Cousin Edith lying on the stable floor in a dead faint.

"Wilbur! Quick!" said Mrs. Pope, and bent over her. Mr. Pope ran across to the harness closet and got out the whiskey. As he bent to administer it, he noticed to his amazement that Copley wasn't paying the slightest attention to what had happened, but had walked over to the easel and was examining the picture on it with little exclamations of pleasure. He looked inquiringly at Mrs. Pope.

"It's beyond me," she whispered. "Look at the pictures."

Mr. Pope looked. Where the putty wharves and all the horrible little boats had been there were now only swirls of paint.

Beneath, one could still make out faintly the outlines of things, but it was as if a whirling hurricane of mist and sleet had swept across the landscape, blurring it almost out of recognition.

He took a quick look at the other pictures. All but those hung highest on the walls were in the same state. Someone . . . He glanced at Ed's stall. Between the cretonne curtains the horse's hind quarters looked indifferent and innocent enough. And yet . . . Wasn't there a certain odd streakiness in the long hairs at the end of his tail?

Cousin Edith was coming to. She opened her eyes and looked up at Mrs. Pope. "Oh, Carlotta," she moaned, "all my nice pictures! Who could have done such a thing? All my months of work ruined—"

"Sssssh!" Mrs. Pope whispered. She glanced round quickly at Mr. Copley, who had gone on to examine with evident relish the three ghouls, who now seemed to have become involved in a monsoon, then stooped and muttered something in Cousin Edith's ear.

Staring incredulously at Mr. Copley's back, Cousin Edith sat up. And as the Popes helped her to the armchair, Mr. Copley turned suddenly. "Really, Miss Manley," he said, "this is extraordinarily fine work! I had no—" He broke off. "Is there anything wrong?"

"No, no," Mrs. Pope said. "Cousin Edith is a little weak; she's—she's just getting over the flu."

Mr. Copley commiserated. Perhaps, he said, another time . . . But Cousin Edith said no, she was quite all right. "Please go on."

"Well," said Mr. Copley, "I'll be frank with you, Miss Manley. I hadn't expected to see anything like this. Such vigorous work! Look at the sweep of those brush strokes!" And he pointed towards the easel. "It's a treatment that is admirably suited to such metropolitan scenes."

"Met—metropolitan?" Cousin Edith stammered. She looked helplessly at Mrs. Pope. "But—"

"My husband and I," said Mrs. Pope quickly, "particularly like this one of the skyscrapers." She pointed to the ghouls.

Mr. Copley nodded. "I was just looking at it. Masterly! The theme so subtly understated, yet so delicately emphasized by these whirling rhythms. Really, Miss Manley, I am amazed!"

"S-so am I," said Cousin Edith. She gripped the arms of

the chair and stared earnestly up at Mr. Copley. Her lips moved several times soundlessly, then she said: "Do you really feel that you could—that you would . . ."

"Of course!" he interrupted. "Oh, decidedly we can do something with these. Too bad there aren't more. Let's see —eight, nine . . . well, enough for a start."

"But those others, above . . ." Cousin Edith pointed towards several of the higher canvases, the only ones that remained as she had originally painted them.

Mrs. Pope cut in with a quick artificial laugh. "Oh now, Cousin Edith!" she said. "Wilbur doesn't really expect you to try to do something with those. He only did them for fun." She turned to Mr. Copley. "Those are my husband's work," she explained.

"Really?" Mr. Copley glanced at them and smiled gently, then he turned his back squarely on Mr. Pope and started making arrangements with Cousin Edith for having her pictures sent in to the gallery. "In a normal year," he said, "we wouldn't think of trying to launch her before fall. But this season is not like other seasons. I think we'll go ahead at once. And you work rather quickly, I imagine; in the fall . . ."

Mr. Pope turned away from them. He slipped a bottle of turpentine into his pocket, then saddled Ed and led him outdoors. But as he put his foot in the stirrup Mrs. Pope came out.

"Wilbur!" she exclaimed under her breath. "What an incredible thing! How could such a thing have happened? My first thought was that somebody had tried to spoil the pictures, but—"

"You want to remember," he said, "that theoretically any change would have been an improvement. I admit I don't see why Copley is so keen on them, but I don't understand this art business anyway. Apparently nowadays the less it looks like anything recognizable the better art it is."

"Yes, but how could it have *happened?*"

"Somnambulism, that's the only possible explanation," said Mr. Pope, inventing on the spur of the moment. "Cousin Edith came out here in her sleep and changed her pictures . . . Oh yes, it's quite a well-known thing. Haven't you read of people who were working on a problem, and then they went to bed, and in the morning they got up and went to their desk and there was the solution, all neatly worked out in their own handwriting?"

"Yes, I've read of it. But in the dark?"

"Curious thing is, they seem quite able to do it in the dark," said Mr. Pope. And he went on to develop his theory. Cousin Edith's subconscious mind was a much better artist than her conscious one. Obviously, it must be, as it couldn't well be worse. And in her sleep it had gone to work and fixed up the pictures. "And you'd better explain that to her, because she's probably pretty confused about the whole thing."

When Mr. Pope and Ed had ridden some distance up a side road, Mr. Pope dismounted and got out his bottle of turpentine and started to clean the paint off the end of Ed's tail.

"Why did you have to stick your nose into things, when they were going along all right?" he demanded. "Copley would have told her the stuff was no good and she'd have gone."

"Yeah, you was right, Wilb," said the horse. "But Copley's just dumb; I still maintain folks would buy those pictures the way they was before I put the finishin' touches onto 'em."

"Well, I told you," Mr. Pope said. "Now we've got her on our hands for Lord knows how long."

"Sure, sure. But ain't it worth something to discover I got so much talent? Cousin Edith and me'd make a good team: she'd do the preliminary spade work, and then I'd back up to the picture and put the art into it with a couple whisks of my talented tail. It kind of—hey, go easy with that turps!—it kind of resigns me to having her around the place."

"Well, I'm glad you're satisfied," said Mr. Pope crossly.

"Look, Wilb," Ed said, "we both of us been too clever for our own good. Me with my tail-swishin' and you with your sleep-walking theory. If you'd shut up she'd have thought that somebody else had been monkeying with 'em, and while she probably wouldn't have said so to Copley, she'd know she couldn't do any more for him. Now she'll think she's some kind of a subconscious genius, and she'll stay here for months, paintin' more, and hopin' she'll fix 'em up in her sleep for Copley."

"I hadn't thought of that," Mr. Pope said. "But I had to produce some explanation. I was afraid Carlotta would notice the paint on your tail."

"Yeah, we both acted for the best," said Ed, "which is always a mistake." He chuckled. "I've played a lot of parts in my time, but I never expected to be cast as the subconscious mind of an old maid."

Mr. Pope said he thought Ed was probably pretty well cast. If what the psychologists say is right, the prim old maids are filled with pretty shocking subconsciousnesses.

"Yeah, none too fragrant, I'm told," said Ed. "But let's not get personal. You know, Wilb, those pictures, the way they are now—they'd puzzle old Freud, wouldn't they? I mean, he'd expect Cousin Edith's subconscious to produce something pretty precise and shocking, instead of a fog. Something like the designs old man Harkness used to make with soap on the mirror behind his bar."

"I thought your friend Harkness ran a livery stable," said Mr. Pope.

"He did. But when the livery business fell off he opened a saloon next door." Ed giggled. "He used to say there was less difference between the two places than you'd believe. He said sometimes he couldn't tell himself which one he was in —same ugly faces, and it smelled just the same. Of course he had some real art in his place—a couple big pictures over the bar—they was much admired."

"I can imagine," Mr. Pope said.

"So can anybody," Ed said. "Same kind of pictures you see in all these here magazines nowadays. In them days art was for the few. The few that had the price of a drink. Then prohibition come in and there wasn't any place for it, saloons being gone, and those pictures was forced into the magazines. Just like drinking was forced into the home."

When Mr. Pope got back from his ride, he found that Cousin Edith had been able to recognize in herself without too much urging a somnambulistic genius. She and Mrs. Pope were still discussing it in the stable. "I didn't really believe that Mr. Copley would want to give me a show after he'd seen my things," she said. "Really I didn't. I always knew my pictures were old-fashioned. Yet I could always appreciate the other things, and wished I could do them. I suppose it's as Carlotta says: when I paint consciously, there are so many inhibitions or something that I sort of tighten up and paint in a kind of finicky way."

"But isn't it wonderful, Cousin Edith," Mr. Pope said, "that Copley is really going to give you a show? And he sells 'em, you know; he's a wonderful salesman."

"Oh, I'm simply too thrilled for words! Of course, Wilbur. But—" She hesitated. "He'll want more pictures," she said.

"I certainly wouldn't worry about that," said Mrs. Pope.

"Sooner or later—tonight, or some night next week—you'll repaint all these others, just as you did the ones he's taking. There's certainly a stronger stimulus to do it now."

"And as you go on," Mr. Pope put in, "your subconscious will free itself more and more. In time you'll be able to do it when you're awake."

"But I'm not sure that I want to," she said. "Oh yes, I know that I *can*—that I *will* do it again. I can tell; I feel it—here." She smote her bosom with a light but dramatic gesture. "To have had a one man show—yes, that has been my ambition. But to go on—to be a professional painter . . . well, it becomes a routine. So many canvases to turn out a year. It isn't as if the money was necessary. I've always been an amateur, and I want to stay one."

"I see what you mean," said Mr. Pope. "You want public appreciation, but not public demand, which can be very exacting. Well, you can always stop."

"I can't now, or he won't have the show. And I can't later; no one ever does. Oh, dear!" wailed Cousin Edith.

This bit of characteristic indecision irritated the Popes, the more as they knew that they were in for—at best—another two months of it. For although Mr. Pope was determined to prevent Cousin Edith's subconscious from doing any more painting even if he had to tie him in his stall, her conscious work would go hopefully on.

"Well," he said heavily, "let's go in and have a drink."

The next morning Mr. Pope was startled by a shriek which seemed to come from the stable. He ran out, and had just reached the door when Cousin Edith, panting and disheveled, burst from it and galloped towards him. She wore a sort of blue kimono thing with pink storks on it, and under one arm was what appeared to be a crushed and rolled up piece of canvas. She caught his arm.

"Oh, Wilbur!" she babbled. "Oh, those dreadful things. It couldn't be me—I couldn't have such awful things in my mind! What will people think?"

Mr. Pope caught her by the shoulders. "Take it easy," he said. "What's the trouble?" He drew her towards the stable door. "What's wrong?"

"Oh, please don't go in there, Wilbur. Oh, after all we've said—"

"But I don't understand," he said. "What's that under your arm?"

She clutched it tighter. "You mustn't see it; nobody must

see it! I'm going in and burn it right away." And she
pulled away from him and made for the house.

Mr. Pope looked after her for a moment, then turned
and went on into the stable. The doors were open. Cousin
Edith, hoping that her subconscious had worked while she
slept, had evidently come out before breakfast and opened
them. The paintings which Ed had put the art into with his
tail were untouched, but of the others, not one but had
suffered alteration into something rich and strange. Cousin
Edith's subconscious had certainly been on the rampage,
and with all inhibitions off. On a road curving down past
one of Cousin Edith's famous putty farmhouses, an auto-
mobile with two figures in it had been rudely drawn with
red paint. The male figure was smoking a pipe, and under-
neath was scrawled "Edith and Harmon." In another picture,
which portrayed a wide stretch of beach, a stout blue nude
reclined grossly on the yellow sand. More nudes, drawn
with a wavering line but great attention to detail, sprawled
in the foreground of other landscapes. The only portrait, that
of a girl in a blue hat, had acquired a moustache. And
there were legends printed across other landscapes: "Edith
loves Harmon," "Wilbur is a stinker," and similar primitive
sentiments.

Mr. Pope was horrified, but he choked back a cackle of
laughter. Then he said: "Ed, come out here."

The horse backed out between the cretonne curtains. He
looked uncertainly at Mr. Pope for a minute, then smirked
and said: "Pretty vulgar display, eh, Wilb? I suppose I ought
to stopped her when she come trailin' out here in her shirt
tail at two this morning and started in, but I got kind of a
scientific interest in these here Freudian manifestations." He
shook his head. "Such a nice folksy old girl she seemed like,
too."

"What was the picture she was taking into the house to
burn?" Mr. Pope asked.

"Boy, she'd certainly burned her brakes out by the time
she got to that one, Wilb!" Ed said. "It was—" He pulled himself up. "Well, I didn't rightly see it—so dark in here and all.
Maybe it's just as well if you didn't either. I expect you'd
kind of like to remember her the way she was. Before her
old subconscious boiled over."

"Remember her?" said Mr. Pope thoughtfully. "Yes, I suppose she'll go now. So I can't kick—is that the idea? Well,
it seems as if you might have taken less drastic measures.

However . . ." He examined the paintings more closely. "I suppose you used a brush?"

"Yeah. Held it in my teeth. It's a different technique than the one I employed before—an entirely different art, really," he said affectedly.

"The difference between your front end and your rear end," said Mr. Pope.

"I can't get them swirling rhythms with a brush," said Ed. "That comes from years of practice swatting flies, I suppose."

Mr. Pope took down the saddle. "Well, we've got to get to the train. Carlotta will have to handle this alone."

There hadn't been much to handle. When Mr. Pope got home that night Cousin Edith was gone, bag and baggage, paints and pictures. Mrs. Pope reported that for once in her life Cousin Edith had shown no indecision. "And the funny thing is," she said, "that after she'd burned that one picture and got over shuddering, I think she was rather, well, pleased with herself."

"She said she didn't want to become a professional."

"Oh, that too, of course. But I mean, pleased to find that she had so much good coarse vulgarity in her. And she still expects to have her show. She sent Copley the ones he liked."

"Did you see the one she burned?" Mr. Pope asked.

"She wouldn't let me."

So presently Mr. Pope went out to the stable and asked Ed about it.

Ed seemed very happy. He pranced up and down, humming: "Wilbur is a stinker; Wilbur is a stinker," until Mr. Pope threatened him with a broom—then he said: "I ain't going to tell you. It's just morbid curiosity on your part." And when Mr. Pope insisted: "Look, Wilb," he said, "there's times in your life when you really got to sock somebody for their own good. And the harder you sock, the kinder it is to the other party in the end. I was awful kind to Cousin Edith, and that's all I'm going to tell you."

And that was all he ever did tell.

A GOLDEN OPPORTUNITY FOR GREAT READING

ALL THE BOOKS YOU'VE ALWAYS WANTED TO READ

THE WORLD'S BEST-SELLING AUTHORS

DON'T MISS THIS OPPORTUNITY TO ORDER THE BESTSELLING BOOKS OF THE YEAR AT LOW, LOW PAPERBACK PRICES

NOVELS, MYSTERIES, WESTERNS, SCIENCE FICTION, CLASSICS, DRAMA, NON-FICTION

NOVELS

☐	N2473—**MILA 18**—Leon Uris	95¢
☐	S2498—**PLOUGH THE SEA**—Robert Wilder	75¢
☐	S2524—**THE KEYS OF THE KINGDOM**—A. J. Cronin	75¢
☐	S2461—**THE WINTER OF OUR DISCONTENT**—John Steinbeck	75¢
☐	S2447—**THE LISTENER**—Taylor Caldwell	75¢
☐	S2433—**SIX O'CLOCK CASUAL**—Clune	75¢
☐	S2432—**THE EDGE OF SADNESS**—Edwin O'Connor	75¢
☐	S2451—**LILITH**—J. R. Salamanca	75¢
☐	S2244—**THE INTERNS**—Richard Frede	75¢
☐	S2130—**THE WAR LOVER**—John Hersey	75¢
☐	H2472—**THE STARS IN THEIR COURSES**—Harry Brown	60¢
☐	H2446—**THE FRAUD**—Paul Rader	60¢
☐	H2428—**BATTLE CRY**—Leon Uris	60¢
☐	H2406—**THE BIG NICKELODEON**—Maritta Wolff	60¢

NON-FICTION

MISCELLANEOUS

CLASSICS

REFERENCE LIBRARY

DUAL LANGUAGE BOOKS

☐ N2479—FAUST, PART 1—Goethe · · · · · · · · · · · · · · · · · · · 95¢
☐ N2482—WERTHER—Goethe · 95¢
☐ N2483—CANDIDE—Voltaire · 95¢

PLEASE NOTE: If you cannot find the titles you want in your local paperback outlet, you may order any of the books listed in this catalog by simply circling the appropriate number below, which corresponds to the number in front of the title. The numbers run horizontally in the same order as the titles appear in the catalog. Then fill out the coupon and mail.

BANTAM BOOKS, INC., DEPT. NY 62
414 East Golf Road, Des Plaines, Illinois
Please send me the Bantam Books circled below.

NAME . . . .

ADDRESS . . . .

CITY . . . .

STATE . . . .

I am enclosing $ . . . . (Check or Money Order—NO CURRENCY PLEASE) SORRY, no C.O.D.'s. NOTE: Please include 10¢ per copy for postage and handling on orders of less than 5 books.

N2473	S2498	S2524	S2461	S2447	S2433	S2432	S2421
S2244	S2130	H2472	H2446	H2428	H2406	H2355	F2475
F2458	F2426	F2417*	F2389	F1946	J2493	J2496	J2489
J2468	J2373	J2362	S2453	H2435	H2424*	F2470	F2465
J2491	J2480*	J2464	J2448	J2442	J2427	J2401	F2462
J2463	A2494	A2477	A2449	F2438	J2484	J2443	J2466
J2436	A2425	DQ2486	DQ2485	DQ2444	S2471	S2452	S2451
S2440	H2476	H2439	F2558	F2495	F2481	J2460	J2419
A2400	NC169	NC151	NC148	SC165	SC162	HC152*	HC120
FC158	FC157	NR35	HR42	HR41	HR39	HR38	HR37
HR44	N2479	N2482	N2483		*Not available in Canada		

ALLOW TWO TO THREE WEEKS FOR DELIVERY
Bantam Books are available at newsstands everywhere